THE DOUBLE SHADOW
AND OTHER FANTASIES

THE DOUBLE SHADOW

AND OTHER FANTASIES

CLARK ASHTON SMITH

WILDSIDE PRESS

THE DOUBLE SHADOW AND OTHER FANTASIES

For more information, contact:

Wildside Press
P.O. Box 301
Holicong, PA 18928-0301 USA
www.wildsidepress.com

CONTENTS

THE VOYAGE
OF KING EUVORAN

The crown of the kings of Ustaim was fashioned only from the rarest materials that could be procured anywhere. The magically graven gold of its circlet had been mined from a huge meteor that fell in the southern isle of Cyntrom, shaking the isle from shore to shore with calamitous earthquake; and the gold was harder and brighter than any native gold of Earth, and was changeable in color from a flamelike red to the yellow of young moons. It was set with thirteen jewels, every one of which was unique and without fellow even in fable. These jewels were a wonder to behold, starring the circlet with strange unquiet fires and fulgurations terrible as the eyes of the cockatrice. But more wonderful than all else was the stuffed gazolba-bird which formed the superstructure of the crown, gripping the circlet with its steely claws above the wearer's brow, and towering royally with resplendent plumage of green, violet and vermilion. Its beak was the hue of burnished brass, its eyes were like small dark garnets in bezels of silver; and seven lacy, miniated quills arose from its ebon-dappled head, and a white tail fell down in a straightly spreading fan like the beams of some white sun behind the circle. The gazolba-bird was the last of its kind, according to the mariners who had slain it in an almost legendary isle beyond Sotar, far to the east of Zothique. For nine generations it had decked the crown of Ustaim, and the kings looked upon it as the sacred emblem of their fortunes, and a talisman inseparable from their royalty, whose loss would be followed by grave disaster.

Euvoran, the son of Karpoom, was the ninth wearer of the crown. Superbly and magnificently he had worn it for two years and ten months, following the death of Karpoom from a surfeit of stuffed eels and jellied salamander's eggs. On all state occasions, levees and daily grantings of public audience and administerings of justice, it had graced the brow of the young king and had conferred upon him a dreadful majesty in the eyes of the beholders. Also, it had served to conceal the lamentable increase of an early baldness.

It came to pass, in the late autumn of the third year of his reign, that King Euvoran rose from a goodly breakfast of twelve courses and twelve wines, and went forth as was his custom to the hall of justice, which occupied an entire wing of his palace in the city of Aramoam, looking down in several-colored marble from its palmy hills to the rippled lazuli of the orient ocean.

Being well fortified by his breakfast, Euvoran felt himself prepared to unravel the most involute skeins of legality and crime, and was likewise ready for the meting of swift punishment to all malefactors. And beside him, at the right arm of his kraken-sculptured throne of ivory, there stood an executioner leaning on a huge mace with a leaden head that was tempered to the hardness of iron. Full often, with this mace, the bones of the more flagitious offenders were broken immediately, or their brains were split in the kings presence on a floor that was strewn with black sand. And beside the left arm of the throne, a professional torturer busied himself continually with the screws and pulleys of certain fearsome instruments of torture, as a warning of their fate to all evil-doers. And not always idle were the turnings of these screws and the tightenings of these pulleys, and not always empty were the metal beds of the machines.

Now, on that morning, the constables of the city brought before King Euvoran only a few petty thieves and suspicious vagrants; and there were no cases of felony such as would have warranted the wielding of the mace or the use of the torture-implements. So the king, who had looked forward to a pleasurable session, was somewhat balked and disappointed; and he questioned with much severity the minor culprits before him, trying to extort from each of them, in turn, an admission of some graver crime than that whereof he was accused. But it seemed that the pilferers were innocent of aught but pilfering; and the vagrants were guilty of naught worse than vagrancy; and Euvoran began to think that the morning would offer scant entertainment. For the bastinado was the heaviest punishment that he could legally impose on such misdemeanants.

"Away with these mackerel!" he roared to the officers, and his crown shook with indignation, and the tall gazolba-bird on the crown appeared to nod and bow. "Away with them, for they pollute my presence. Give each of them a hundred strokes with the hardwood briar on the bare sole of each foot, and forget not the heels. Then drive them forth from Aramoam toward the public refuse-grounds, and prod them with red-hot tridents if they linger in their crawling."

Then, ere the officers could obey him, there entered the hall of justice two belated constables, haling between them a peculiar and most unsavory individual with the long-handled, many pointed hooks that were used in Aramoam for the apprehending of malefactors and suspects. And though the hooks were seemingly embedded in his flesh as well as the filthy rags that served him for raiment, the prisoner bounded perpetually aloft in the manner of a goat, and his captors were obliged to follow in these lively and undignified saltations, so that the three presented the appearance of tumblers. With a final volitation in which the officers were drawn through the air like the tails of a kite, the incredible personage came to a pause before Euvoran. The king regarded him in amazement, blinking rapidly, and was not prepossessed by the singular suppleness with which he louted to the very floor, upsetting the scarce-recovered equilibrium of the officers, and causing them to sprawl at full length in the royal presence.

"Ha! What have we now?" said the king in an ominous voice.

"Sire, 'tis another vagabond," replied the breathless officers, when they had regained a more respectfully inclined position. "He would have passed through Aramoam by the main avenue in the fashion that you behold, without stopping, and without even lessening the altitude of his saltations, if we had not arrested him."

"Such behavior is highly suspicious," growled Euvoran hopefully. "Prisoner, declare your name, your nativity and occupation, and the infamous crimes of which, beyond doubt, you are guilty."

The captive, who was cross-eyed, appeared to regard Euvoran, the royal mace-wielder, and the royal torturer and his instruments all in a single glance. He was ill-favored to an extravagant degree; his nose, ears and other features were all possessed of unnatural mobility; and he grimaced perpetually in a manner that caused his unclean beard to toss and curl like seaweed on a boiling whirlpool.

"I have many names," he replied, in an insolent voice whose pitch was peculiarly disagreeable to Euvoran, setting his teeth on edge like the grating of metal on glass. "As for my nativity and occupation, the knowledge of these, O king, would profit you little."

"Sirrah, you are malapert. Give answer or tongues of red-hot iron shall question you," roared Euvoran.

"Be it known to you, then, that I am a necromancer, and was born in the realm where the dawn and the sunset come together and the moon is equal in brightness to the sun."

"Ha! A necromancer!" snorted the king. "Know you not that necromancy is a capital crime in Ustaim? Verily, we shall find means to dissuade you from the practice of such infamies."

At a sign from Euvoran, the officers drew their captive toward the instruments of torture. Much to their surprise, in view of his former ebullience, he allowed himself to be chained supinely on the iron bed that produced a remarkable elongation of the limbs of its occupants. The official engineer of these miracles began to work the levers, and the bed lengthened little by little with a surly grating, till it seemed that the prisoner's joints would be torn apart. Inch by inch was added to his stature; and though, after a time, he had gained more than a half-cubit from the stretching, he appeared to experience no discomfort whatever; and to the stupefaction of all present, it became plain that the elasticity of his arms, legs and body was beyond the extensibility of the rack itself; for the latter was now drawn to its limits.

All were silent, viewing this prodigy; and Euvoran rose from his seat and went over to the rack, as if doubtful of his own eyes that testified to a thing so enormous. And the prisoner said to him:

"It were well to release me, O King Euvoran."

"Say you so?" the king cried out in a rage. "However, it is not thus that we deal with felons in Ustaim." And he made a private sign to the executioner, who came forward quickly, rearing his massive, leaden-headed mace aloft.

"On your own head be it," said the necromancer, and he rose instantly from the iron bed, breaking the bonds that held him, as if they had been chains of grass. Then, towering to a terrible height, which the wrenchings of the rack had given him, he pointed his long forefinger, dark and sere as that of a mummy, at the king's crown; and simultaneously he uttered a foreign word that was shrill and eldritch as the crying of migrant fowl that pass over toward unknown shores in the night. And lo! As if in answer to that word, there was a loud, sudden flapping of wings above Euvoran's head and the king felt that his brow was lightened by the crown's goodly and well-accustomed weight. A shadow fell upon him, and he, and all who were present, beheld above them in the air the stuffed gazolba-bird, which had been slain more than two hundred years before by sea-faring men in a remote isle. The wings of the bird, a living splendor, were outspread as if for flight, and it carried still in its steely claws the rare circlet of the crown. Librating, it hung for a little over the throne, while the king watched it in wordless awe and consternation. Then, with metallic whirring, its white tail deployed like the beams of a flying sun, it flew swiftly through the open portals, and passed seaward from Aramoam into the morning light.

After it, with great bounds and goatish leapings, the necromancer followed; and no man tried to deter him. But those who saw him depart from the city swore that he went north along the ocean-strand, while the bird flew directly eastward, as if homing to the half-fabulous isle of its nativity. Thereafter, as if he had gone at a single bound into alien realms, the necromancer was not seen in Ustaim. But the crew of a merchant galley from Sotar, landing later in Aramoam, told how the gazolba-bird had passed over them in mid-main, a several-colored glory still flying toward the sources of the dayspring. And they said that the crown of changeable gold, with its thirteen fellowless gems, was still carried by the bird. And though they had trafficked long in the archipelagoes of wonder, and had seen many prodigies, they deemed this thing a most rare and unexampled portent.

King Euvoran, so strangely reft of that avian head-gear, with his baldness rudely bared to the gaze of thieves and vagrants in the hall of justice, was as one on whom the gods have sent down a sudden bolt. If the sun had turned black in heaven, or his palace walls had crumbled about him, his dumbfoundment would hardly have been more excessive. For it seemed to him that his royalty had flown with that crown which was the emblem and the talisman of his fathers. And, moreover, the thing was wholly against nature, and the laws of god and man were annulled thereby: since never before, in all history or fable, had a dead bird taken flight from the kingdom of Ustaim.

Indeed, the loss was a dire calamity, and Euvoran, having donned a voluminous turban of purple samite, held council with the sagest ministers regarding the state dilemma that had thus arisen. The ministers were no less troubled and perplexed than the king: for the bird and the circlet were both irreplaceable. And in the meanwhile, the rumor of this misfortune was borne abroad through Ustaim, and the land became filled with lamentable doubt and confusion, and some of the people began to murmur covertly against Euvoran, saying that no man could be the rightful ruler of that country without the gazolba-crown.

Then, as was the custom of the kings in a time of national exigence, Eurovan repaired to the temple in which dwelt the god Geol, who was a terrestrial god and the chief deity of Aramoam. Alone, with bare head and unshod feet, as was ordained by hierarchal law, he entered the dim adytum where the image of Geol, potbellied, and wrought of earth-brown faience, reclined eternally on its back and regarded the motes in a narrow beam of sunlight from the slotted wall. And, falling prone in the dust that had gathered around the idol through ages, the king gave homage to Geol, and implored an oracle to illuminate and guide him in his need. And after an interim, a voice issued from the god's navel, as if a subterrene rumbling had become articulate. And the voice said to King Eurovan:

"Go forth and seek the gazolba in those isles that lie beneath the orient sun. There, O king, on the far coasts of dawn, thou shalt again behold the living bird which is the symbol and the fortune of thy dynasty; and there, with thine own hand, thou shalt slay the bird."

Euvoran was much comforted by this oracle, since the utterances of the god were deemed infallible. And it seemed to him that the oracle implied in plain terms that he should recover the lost crown of Ustaim, which had the reanimated bird for its superstructure. So, returning to the royal palace, he sent for the captains of his proudest argosies of war, which lay then at anchor in the tranquil harbor of Aramoam, and ordered them to make immediate provision for a long voyage into the east and among the archipelagoes of morning.

When all was made ready, King Euvoran went aboard the flagship of the fleet, which was a towering quadrireme with oars of beef-wood and sails of stout woven byssus dyed in yellowish scarlet, and a long gonfalon at the mast head, bearing the gazolba bird in its natural colors on a field of heavenly cobalt. The rowers and sailors of the quadrireme were mighty Negroes from the north; and the soldiers who manned it were fierce mercenaries from Xylac in the west; and with him, going aboard, the king took certain of his concubines and jesters and other ministrants, as well as an ample store of liquors and rare viands, so that he should lack for nothing during the voyage. And mindful of the prophecy of Geol, the king armed himself with a longbow and a quiver filled with parrot-feathered arrows; and he also carried a sling of lion-leather and a blowgun of black bamboo from which tiny poisoned darts were discharged.

It seemed that the gods favored the voyage; for a wind blew strongly from the west on the morning of the departure; and the fleet, which numbered fifteen vessels, was borne with bellying sails toward the sea-risen sun. And the farewell clamors and shoutings of Euvoran's people on the wharves were soon stilled by distance; and the marble houses of Aramoam on its four palmy hills here drowned in that swiftly foundering bank of azure which was the shoreline of Ustaim. And, thereafter, for many days, the iron-wood beaks of the galleys clove a softly weltering sea of indigo that rose unbroken on all sides to a cloudless, dark-blue heaven.

Trusting in the oracle of Geol, that earthen god who had never failed his fathers, the king made merry as was his wont; and reclining beneath a saffron canopy on the poop of the quadrireme, he swilled from an emerald beaker the wines and brandies that had lain in his palace-vaults, storing the warmth of elder, ardent suns whereon oblivion's black rime was fallen. And he laughed at the ribaldries of his fools, at unquenchable ancient bawdries that had won the laughter of other kings in the sea-lost continents of yore. And his women diverted him with harlotries that were older than Rome or Atlantis. And ever he kept at hand, beside his couch, the weapons wherewith he hoped to hunt and slay again the gazolba-bird, according to the oracle of Geol.

The winds were unfailing and auspicious, and the fleet sped onward, with the great black oarsmen singing gaily at their oars, and the gorgeous sailcloths flapping loudly, and the long banners floating on the air like straight-blown flames. After a fortnight they came to Sotar, whose low-lying coasts of cassia and sago barred the sea for a hundred leagues from north to south; and in Loithe, the chief port, they paused to inquire for the gazolba-bird. There were rumors that the bird had passed above Sotar; and some of the people said that a cunning sorcerer of that isle, named Iffibos, had drawn it down through his sorcery and had closed it in a cage of sandalwood. So the king landed in Loithe, deeming his quest perhaps already nigh to its end, and went with certain of his captains and soldiers to visit Iffibos, who dwelt in a retired vale among the mountains at the island's core.

It was a tedious journey, and Euvoran was much annoyed by the huge and vicious gnats of Sotar, which were no respecters of royalty, and were

THE VOYAGE OF KING EUVORAN ∞ 17

always insinuating themselves under his turban. And when, after some delay and divagation in the deep jungle, he came to the house of Iffibos on a high, precarious crag, he found that the bird was merely one of the bright-plumaged vultures peculiar to the region, which Iffibos had tamed for his own amusement. So the king returned to Loithe, after declining somewhat rudely the invitation of the sorcerer, who wished to show him the unusual feats of falconry to which he had trained the vulture. And in Loithe the king tarried no longer than was needful for the laying aboard of fifty jars of the sovereign arrack in which Sotar excels all other lands.

Then, coasting the southern cliffs and promontories, where the sea bellowed prodigiously in mile-deep caverns, the ships of Euvoran sailed beyond Sotar, and Tosk, whose people were more akin to apes and lemurs than to men. And Euvoran asked the people for news of the gazolba, and received only a chattering as of apes in answer. So the king ordered his men-at-arms to catch a number of these savage islanders and crucify them on the coco-palms for their incivility. And the men-at-arms pursued the nimble people of Tosk for a full day among the trees and boulders in which the isle abounded, but without catching a single one of them. So the king contented himself by crucifying several of the men-at-arms for their failure to obey him and sailed on to the seven atolls of Yumatot, whose inhabitants were mostly cannibals. And beyond Yumatot, which was the usual limit of eastern voyaging from Ustaim, the vessels entered the Ilozian Sea, and began to touch at partly mythic shores and islands charted only in story.

It were tedious to relate the full particulars of that voyage, in which Euvoran and his captains went ever toward the sources of the dawn.

Various and without number were the strange marvels they found in the archipelagoes beyond Yumatot; but nowhere could they find a single feather such as had formed part of the gazolba's plumage; and the quaint people of those isles had never seen the bird.

Howbeit, the king beheld many a flock of unknown, fiery-winged fowl that went over the galleys in mid-sea, passing between the unmarked islets. And, landing often, he practiced his archery on lorikeets and lyre-birds and boobies, or stalked the golden cockatoos with his blowgun. And he chased the dodo and dinornis on shores that were otherwise unpeopled. And once, in a sea of high-beetling barren rocks, the fleet was assailed by mighty griffins that flew down from their crag-built eyries, with wings shining like feathery brass under the meridian sun, and making a harsh clangor as of shields shaken in battle. And the griffins, being both fero-cious and pertinacious, were driven away with much difficulty by boulders hurled from the catapults of the vessels.

Everywhere, as the ships drove eastward, there were multitudes of fowl. But at the sunset of a day in the fourth moon following their depar-ture from Aramoam, the vessels approached a nameless isle that towered mile-high with cliffs of black, naked basalt, around whose base the sea cried with baffled anger, and about whose precipices there were no wings nor voices of birds. The isle was topped with gnarly cypresses that might have grown in a windy graveyard; and sullenly it took the afterglow, as if drenched with a gore of darkening blood. Far up in the cliffs there were strange columned eaves like the dwellings of forgotten troglodytes, but seemingly inaccessible to men; and the caves to all appearances were unoc-cupied by any kind of life, though pitting the face of the isle for leagues.

And Euvoran ordered his captains to drop anchor, meaning to search for a landing-place on the morrow: since, in his anxiety to retrieve the gazolba, he would pass no isle of the dawnward main, not even the unlikeliest, without due inquiry and examination.

Quickly fell the darkness, without moon, till the close-anchored ships were visible to each other only by their lanterns. And Euvoran sat at supper in his cabin, sipping the golden arrack of Sotar between mouthfuls of mango-jelly and phenicopter's meat. And, saving a small watch on each of the vessels, the sailors and men-at-arms were all at evening mess; and the rowers ate their figs and lentils in the oar-decks. Then, from the watches, there was a wild shouting of alarm, and the shouting ceased in a moment, and each of the vessels rocked and sagged in the water, as if a monstrous weight had settled upon it. No man knew the thing that had happened, but everywhere there was turmoil and confusion, some saying that the fleet was attacked by pirates. Those who peered from the ports and oar-holes saw that the lanterns of their neighbors had been quenched, and perceived a milling and seething as of low-driven clouds in the darkness, and saw that foul black creatures, large as men and winged like oupires, were clinging to the ranged oars in myriads. And those who dared to approach the open hatches found that the decks, the rigging and the masts were crowded with similar creatures, who, it seemed, were of nocturnal habit and had come down in the manner of bats from their caves in the island.

Then, like things of nightmare, the monsters began to invade the hatches and assail the ports, clawing with hellish talons at the men who opposed them. And, being somewhat hampered by their wings, they were driven back with spears and arrows, but returned again and again in a thickening press without number, cheeping with a faint and bat-like sound. It was plain that they were vampires, for whenever they had dragged a man down, as many of them as could gain mouthhold would fasten on him incontinently, and suck his blood till little more remained than a skinful of bones. The upper oar-decks, being half open to the sky, were quickly usurped, and their crews overcome with a hideous swarming; and the rowers in the orlops cried that the sea-water was pouring in through the oar-holes as the ships sank deeper beneath an ever-gathering weight.

All night, at the ports and hatches, the men of Euvoran fought the vampires, taking turns in shifts when they wearied. Many of them were seized and their blood sucked before the eyes of their fellows as the night wore on; and the vampires, it seemed, were not to be slain by mortal weapons, though the blood they had gorged came forth in spouting rills from their wounded bodies. And thicklier they clustered upon the fleet, till the biremes began to founder, and the rowers were drowned in the sunken lower decks of certain triremes and quadriremes.

King Euvoran was wroth at this unseemly turmoil that had inter-rupted his supper; and when the golden arrack was spilt and the dishes of rare meat were emptied on the floor by the vessel's violent rocking, he would have issued from his cabin, fully armed, to try conclusions with these piacular miscreants. But, even as he turned to fling wide the cabin-door, there was a soft infernal pittering at the port-holes behind him; and the women who were with him began to shriek, and the fools cried out in terror. And the king saw in the lamplight a grisly face with the teeth and nostrils of a flittermouse, that leaned in through one of the cabin-ports. He sought to repel the face, and thereafter, till dawn, he fought the vampires with those very weapons he had designed for the slaying of the gazolba; and the ship's captain, who was with him at supper, guarded a second port with his claymore; and the others were held by two of the king's eunuchs, armed with scimitars. In this warfare they were favored by the smallness of the ports, which could hardly in any case have allowed the free passage of their winged assailants. And, after lightless hours of tedious, horrid struggle, the darkness became thinned with brown twilight, and the vampires lifted from the vessels in a black cloud and returned to their caves in the mile-high cliffs of that unnamed island.

Heavy was the heart of Euvoran within him when he surveyed the damage done to his proud argosies of war: for, among the fifteen vessels, seven had sunk in the night, borne under and swamped by those obscenely clinging hordes of oupires; and the decks of the others were bloody as abbatoirs; and half of the sailors and rowers and men-at-arms were lying flat and flaccid as empty wineskins after the greedy drinking of the great bats. And the sails and banners were shredded into rags; and everywhere, from beak to rudder of Euvoran's galleys, there was the stain and reek of a Stymphalian foulness. So, lest another eve should find them within wing-shot of that accursed isle, the king ordered his remaining captains to weigh anchor; and the other ships, with sea-water still awash in their orlops, and some with drowned rowers still at the oars of their nether banks, drew slowly and heavily to eastward, till the pitted walls of the isle began to sink beneath the main. At eve there was no land in sight anywhere; and after two days, still unharried by the vampires, they came to a coral island, low in the wave, with a calm lagoon that was haunted only by ocean-fowl. And there, for the first time, Euvoran paused to repair his tattered sails, and pump the sea from his holds, and clean the blood and vileness from his decks.

However, in spite of this disaster, the king abated not in any degree his purpose, to sail ever on toward the fountains of the day, until, as Geol had predicted, he should come again on the flown gazolba and slay it with his own royal hand. So, for another moon, they passed amid other and stranger archipelagoes, and penetrated deeplier into the regions of myth and story.

Bravely they drove into mornings of amaranth crossed by gilded lories, and noontides of darkly ardent sapphire where the rose flamingoes went before them to lost, inviolate strands. The stars changed above them, and under the alien-figured Signs they heard the wild, melancholy crying of swans that flew southward fleeing the winter of realms indiscoverable, and seeking the summer in trackless worlds. And they held speech with fabulous men who wore for mantles the ell-wide pennons of the roc, trailing far on the earth behind them; and men who arrayed themselves in apyornis plumes. And they spoke also with antic people whose bodies were covered with a down like that of a new-hatched fowl, and others whose flesh was studded as if with pin-feathers. But nowhere could they learn aught of the gazolba.

At mid-forenoon, early in the sixth month of the voyage, a new and unheard-of shore ascended from the deep, curving for many miles, from northeast to southwest, with sheltered harbors, and cliffs and pinnacled crags that were interspaced with low-lying verdurous dales. As the galleys hove toward it, Euvoran and his captains saw that towers were built on certain of the highmost crags; but in the haven below them there were no ships at anchor nor boats moving; and the shore of the haven was a wilderness of green trees and grass. And, sailing still nearer, and entering the harbor, they descried no evident sign of man, other than the crag-reared towers.

The place, however, was full of an extraordinary number and variety of birds, ranging in size from little tits and passerines to creatures of greater wingspread than eagle or condor. They circled the ships in coveys and great, motley flocks, seeming to be both curious and wary; and Euvoran saw that a winged concourse, as it were, went to and fro above the woods and about the cliffs and towers. He bethought him that here was a likely haunt in which to track down the gazolba; so, arming himself for the chase, he went ashore in a small boat with several of his men.

The birds, even the largest, were patently timid and inoffensive; for when the king landed on the beach, the very trees appeared to take flight, so numerous were the fowl that soared and flew inland, or sought the crags and pinnacles that rose beyond bow-shot. None remained of the multitude visible shortly before; and Euvoran marvelled at such cunning; and moreover he was somewhat exasperated, for he wished not to depart without bringing down a trophy of his skill, even though he should fail to find the gazolba itself. And he deemed the behavior of the birds all the more curious because of the island's solitude: for here there were no paths other than would be made by forest animals; and the woods and meadows were wholly wild and incult; and the towers were seemingly desolate, with seafowl and land-fowl flying in and out of their empty windows.

The king and his men combed the deserted woods along the shore, and came to a steep slope of bushes and dwarf cedars, whose upper incline approached the tallest tower at one side. Here, at the slope's bottom,

Euvoran saw a small owl that slept in one of the cedars, as if wholly unaware of the commotion made by the other birds in their flight. And Euvoran trained an arrow and shot down the owl, though ordinarily he would have spared a prey so paltry. And he was about to pick up the fallen owl, when one of the men who accompanied him cried out as if in alarm. Then, turning his head as he stooped beneath the foliage of the cedar, the king beheld a brace of colossal birds, larger than any he had yet descried on that isle, who came down from the tower like falling thunderbolts. Before he could fit another arrow to the string, they were upon him with the drumming of their mighty vans, and beating him instantly to the ground, so that he was aware of them only as a storm of dreadfully rushing plumes and a hurlyburly of cruel beaks and talons. And, before his men could rally to assist him, one of the birds fastened its huge claws in the shoulder-cape of the king's mantle, not sparing the flesh beneath in its fell clutch, and carried him away to the tower on the crag as easily as a ger-falcon would have carried a small leveret. The king was wholly helpless, and he had dropped his longbow beneath the onset of the birds, and his blowgun had been shaken loose from the girdle at which it depended, and all his darts and arrows were spilled. And he had no weapon remaining, other than a sharp misericordia; and this he could not use to any purpose against his captor in mid-air.

Swiftly he neared the tower, with a flock of lesser fowl circling about him and shrieking as if with derision till he was deafened by their din. And a sickness came upon him because of the height to which he had been carried and the violence of his ascent; and giddily he saw the walls of the tower sink past him with wide and portal-like windows. Then, as he began to retch in his sickness, he was borne in through one of the windows and was dropped rudely on the floor of a high and spacious chamber.

He sprawled at full length on his face and lay vomiting for awhile, heedless of his surroundings. Then, recovering somewhat, he raised himself to a sitting position, and beheld before him, above a sort of dais, an enormous perch of red gold and yellow ivory wrought in the form of a new crescent arching upward. The perch was supported between posts of black jasper flecked as if with blood, and upon it there sat a most gigantic and uncommon bird, eyeing Euvoran with a grim and dreadful and austere mien, as an emperor might eye the gutter-scum that his guards have haled before him for some obscene offense. The plumage of the bird was Tyrian purple, and his beak was like a mighty pick-ax of pale bronze that darkened greenly toward the point, and he clutched the perch with iron talons that were longer than the mailed fingers of a warrior. His head was adorned with quills of turquoise blue and amber yellow, like many a pointed crown; and about his long, unfeathered throat, rough as the scaled skin of a dragon, he wore a singular necklace composed of human heads, and the heads of various ferine beasts such as the weasel, the wildcat, the stoat and the fox, all of which had been reduced to a common size and were no larger than groundnuts.

Euvoran was terrified by the aspect of this fowl; and his alarm was not lessened when he saw that many other birds of a size inferior only to his were sitting about the chamber on less costly and less elevated perches, even as grandees of the realm might sit in the presence of their sovereign. And behind Euvoran, like guards, there stood together with its fellow the creatures that had rapt him to the tower.

Now, adding to his utter confounding, the great Tyrian-feathered bird addressed him in human speech. And the bird said to him in a harsh but magniloquent and majestic voice:

"Too hardily, O filth of mankind, thou hast intruded on the peace of Ornava, isle that is sacred to the birds, and wantonly thou hast slain one of my subjects. For know that I am the monarch of all birds that fly, walk, wade or swim on this terraqueous globe of Earth; and in Ornava is my seat and my capital. Verily, justice shall be done upon thee for thy crime. But if thou hast aught to say in thy defence, I will give thee hearing now, for I would not that even the vilest of earthly vermin, and the most pernicious, should accuse me of inequity or tyranny."

Then, blustering somewhat, though sorely afraid at heart, Euvoran gave answer to the bird, and said:

"I came hither seeking the gazolba, which adorned my crown in Ustaim, and was feloniously reft from me together with the crown through the spell of a lawless necromancer. And know that I am Euvoran, King of Ustaim, and I bow me to no bird, not even the mightiest of that species."

Thereat the ruler of the birds, as if amazed and more indignant than before, made question of Euvoran and interrogated him sharply concerning the gazolba. And, learning that this bird had been slain by sailors and afterwards stuffed, and that the whole purpose of Euvoran in his voyage was to catch and kill it a second time and re-stuff it if necessary, the ruler cried in a great and wrathful voice:

"This helpeth not thy case but showeth thee guilty of a twofold and a triple infamy: for thou hast owned a most abominable thing and one that subverteth nature. In this my tower, as is right and proper, I keep the bodies of men that my taxidermists have stuffed for me; but truly, it is not allow-able nor sufferable that man should do thus to birds. So, for the sake of justice and retribution, I shall presently commit thee to one of my taxider-mists. Indeed, methinks that a stuffed king (since even the vermin have kings) will serve to enhance my collection."

After that, he addressed Euvoran's guards and enjoined them: "Away with this vileness. Confine it to the man-cage, and maintain a strict watch before it."

Euvoran, urged and directed by the pecking of his guards, was compelled to climb a sort of sloping ladder with broad rungs of teak, that led from the chamber to one above it in the tower's top. In the center of this room there was a bamboo cage of capacity more than ample for the housing of six men. The king was driven into the cage, and the birds bolted the door upon him with their claws, which seemed to have the deftness of fingers. Thereafter one of them remained by the cage, eyeing Euvoran vigi-lantly through the spaces of the bars; and the other flew away through a great window and did not return.

The king sat down on a litter of straw, since the cage contained no better provision for his comfort. Despair was heavy upon him, and it seemed that his plight was both dreadful and ignominious. And sorely was he astonished, that a bird should speak with human speech, insulting and reviling humankind; and he deemed it an equally monstrous thing that a bird should dwell in royal state, with servitors to do his will, and the pomp and power of a king. And, pondering these unholy prodigies, Euvoran waited for his doom in the man-cage; and after awhile, water and raw grain were brought to him in earthen vessels; but he could not eat the grain. And

still later, as the day drew toward afternoon, he heard a shouting of men
and a shrieking of birds below the tower; and above these noises, anon,
there were clashings as of weapons and thuddings as of boulders loosened
from the crag. So Euvoran knew that his sailors and soldiers, having seen
him borne into captivity in the tower, were assailing the place in an effort
to succor him. And the noises waxed, mounting to a most tremendous and
atrocious din, and there were cries as of people mortally wounded, and a
vengeful shrilling as of harpies in battle. Then, presently, the clamor ebbed
away, and the shoutings grew faint, and Eurovan knew that his men had
failed to take the tower. And hope waned within him, dying in a darker
murk of despair.

So the afternoon went over, declining seaward, and the sun touched
Euvoran with its level beams through a western window and colored the
bars of his cage with a mockery of gold. Presently, the light flowed from the
room, and after awhile the twilight rose, weaving a tremulous phantom
web of the pale air. And between the sunset and the darkness, a night-guard
came in to relieve the day-flying owl who warded the captive king. The
newcomer was a nyctalops with glowing yellow eyes, and he stood taller
that Euvoran himself, and was formed and feathered somewhat in the
burly fashion of an owl, and he had the stout legs of a megapode. Euvoran
was uncomfortably aware of the bird's eyes, which burned upon him with a
brighter bale as the dusk deepened. Hardly could he sustain that ever vigilant scrutiny. But anon the moon rose, being but little past the full, and
poured a spectral quicksilver into the room, and paled the eyes of the bird;
and Euvoran conceived a desperate plan.

His captors, deeming all his weapons lost, had neglected to remove from his girdle the misericordia, which was long and double-edged and needle-sharp at the tip. And stealthily he gripped the hilt of his misericordia under his mantle, and feigned a sudden illness with groanings and tossings and convulsions that threw him against the bars. And, even as he had schemed, the great nyctalops came nearer, curious to learn what ailed the king; and stooping, he leaned his owl-like head between the bars above Euvoran. And the king, pretending a more violent convulsion, drew the misericordia from its sheath and struck quickly at the outstretched throat of the bird.

Shrewdly the thrust went home, piercing the deepest veins, and the squawking of the bird was choked by his own blood; and he fell, flapping noisily, so that Euvoran feared that all the occupants of the tower would be awakened by the sound. But it seemed that his fears were bootless; for none came to the chamber; and soon the flappings ceased, and the nyctalops lay still in a great heap of ruffled feathers. Thereupon the king proceeded with his plan, and shot back the bolts of the wide-latticed bamboo door with small difficulty. Then, going to the head of the teak-wood ladder which ran to the room beneath, he looked down and beheld the ruler of the birds asleep in the moonlight on his chryselephantine perch, with his terrible pick-ax beak under his wing. And Euvoran was afraid to descend into the chamber, lest the ruler should awake and see him. And also, it occurred to him that the lower stories of the tower might well be guarded by such fowl as the nocturnal creature he had slain.

Again his despair returned upon him; but being of a sleightful and crafty bent, Euvoran bethought him of another scheme. With much labor, using the misericordia, he skinned the mighty nyctalops, and cleaned the blood from its plumage as best he could. Then Euvoran wrapped himself in the skin, with the head of the nyctalops rearing above his own head, and eyeholes in its burly throat through which he could look out amidst the feathers. And the skin fitted him well enough because of his pigeon-breast and his potbelly; and his spindle shanks were hidden behind the heavy shanks of the bird as he walked.

Then, imitating the gait and carriage of this fowl, the king descended the ladder, treading cautiously to avoid a fall and making little noise, lest the ruler of the birds should awaken and detect his imposture. And the ruler was all alone, and he slept without stirring while Euvoran reached the floor and crossed the chamber stealthily to another ladder, leading to the next room below.

In this room there were many great birds asleep on perches, and the king was nigh to perishing with terror as he passed among them. Some of the birds moved a little and chirped drowsily, as if aware of his presence; but none challenged him. And he went down into a third room, and was startled to see therein the standing figures of many men, some in the garb of sailors, and others clad like merchants, and others nude and ruddled with bright ores like savages. And the men were still and stark as if enchanted; and the king feared them little less than he had feared the birds. But remembering that which the ruler had told him, he divined that these were persons who had been captured even as he himself, and had been slain by the birds and preserved through the art of an avian taxidermy. And, trembling, he passed down to another room, which was full of stuffed cats and tigers and serpents and various other enemies of birdkind. And the room below this was the ground story of the tower, and its windows and portals by several gigantic night-fowl similar to that whose skin was worn by the king. Here, indeed, was his greatest peril and the supreme trial of his courage; for the birds eyed him alertly with their fiery golden orbs, and they greeted him with a soft whoo-whooing as of owls. And the knees of Euvoran knocked together behind the bird-shanks; but, imitating the sound in reply, he passed among the guards and was not molested by them. And, reaching an open portal of the tower, he saw the moonlight rock of the crag lying at a distance of no more than two cubits below him; and he hopped from the doorsill in the manner of a fowl, and found his way precariously from ledge to ledge along the crag, till he reached the upper beginning of that declivity at whose bottom he had slain the little owl. Here his descent was easier, and he came anon to the woods around the harbor.

But, ere he could enter the woods, there was a shrill singing of arrows about him, and the king was wounded slightly by one of the arrows, and he roared out in anger, and dropped the mantling birdskin. Thereby, no doubt, he was saved from death at the hands of his own men, who were coming through the woods with intent to assail the tower at night. And, learning this, the king forgave the jeopardy in which their arrows had placed him. But he thought it best to refrain from attacking the tower, and to quit the isle with all dispatch. So returning to his flagship, he ordered all his captains to set sail immediately; for, knowing the baleful power of the bird-monarch, he was more than apprehensive of pursuit; and he deemed it well to place a wide interval of sea between his vessels and that isle ere dawn. So the galleys drew from the tranquil harbor, and rounding a north-eastern promontory, they went due east in a course contrary to the moon.

And, Euvoran, sitting in his cabin, regaled himself with a variety and pleni-tude of viands to make up for his fasting in the man-cage; and he drank a whole gallon of palm-wine and added thereto a jarful of the puissant pale-gold arrack of Sotar.

Halfway betwixt midnight and morn, when the isle of Ornava was left far behind, the steersmen of the vessels beheld a wall of ebon cloud that rose swiftly athwart the heavens, spreading and toppling in towers of thunder, till the storm overtook Euvoran's fleet and drove it on as if with the loosed hurricanes of hell through a welter of unstarred chaos. The ships were sundered in the gloom and were borne far apart; and at daybreak the king's quadrireme was alone in a prone-rushing tumult of mingled wave and cloud; and the mast was shattered, along with most of the beef-wood oars; and the vessel was a toy for the demons of the tempest.

For three days and nights, with no glimmer of sun or star discerned through the ever-boiling murk, the vessel was hurled onward as if caught in a cataract of elements pouring to some bottomless gulf beyond the fringes of the world. And early on the fourth day the clouds were somewhat riven; but a wind still blew like the breath of perdition. Then, lifting darkly through the spray and vapor, a half-seen land arose before the prow, and the helmsman and the rowers were wholly helpless to turn the doomed ship from its course. And shortly after, with a great crashing of its carven beak, and a terrible rending of timbers, the vessel struck on a low reef hidden by the flying foam, and its lower decks were flooded quickly. And the vessel began to founder, with the poop tilting sharply and more sharply, and the water frothing at the lee bulwarks.

Gaunt and cragged and austere was the shore beyond the reef, beheld only through the veils of the sea's foaming fury. And scant, it seemed, was the hope of reaching land. But, ere the wrecked argosy had gone beneath him, Euvoran lashed himself with ropes of coir to an empty wine-barrel, and cast himself from the sloping deck. And those of his men who were not already drowned in the hold or swept overboard by the typhoon, leapt after him into that high wallowing sea, some trusting only to their might as swimmers and others clinging to casks or broken spars or planks. And most were drawn under in the seething maelstroms or were beaten to death on the rocks; and of all the ship's company, the king alone survived and was cast ashore with the breath of life unquenched within him by the bitter sea.

Half-drowned and senseless, he lay where the surf had spewed him on a shelving beach. Soon the gale forgot its violence, and the billows came in with falling crests, and the clouds went over in a rack of pearl, and the sun, climbing above the rock, shone down upon Euvoran from a deep immaculate azure. And the king, still dazed from the buffeting rudeness of the sea, heard dimly and as if in a dream the shrilling of an unknown bird. Then, opening his eyes, he beheld betwixt himself and the sun, librating on spread wings, that various-colored glory of plumes and feathers which he knew as the gazolba. Crying again with a voice that was harsh and shrill as that of the peafowl, the bird hung above him for a moment, and then flew inland through a rift among the crags.

Forgetful of all his hardships and the loss of his proud galleys of war, the king unbound himself in haste from the empty barrel; and, rising giddily, he followed the bird. And, though he was now weaponless, it seemed to him that the fulfillment of the oracle of Geol was at hand. And hopefully he armed himself with a great cudgel of driftwood and gathered heavy pebbles from the beach as he pursued the gazolba.

Beyond the cleft in the high and rugged crags, he found a sheltered valley with quiet-flowing springs, and woods of exotic leaf, and fragrant orient shrubs in blossom. Here, from bough to bough before his astounded eyes, there darted great numbers of fowl that wore the gaudy plumage of the gazolba; and among them he was unable to distinguish the one he had followed, deeming it the avian garniture of his lost crown. The multitude of these birds was a thing beyond his comprehension: since he and all his people had thought the stuffed fowl unique and fellowless throughout the world, even as the other components of the crown of Ustaim. And it came to him that his fathers had been deceived by the mariners who had slain the birds in a remote isle, swearing later that it was the last of its kind.

However, though wrath and confusion were in his heart, Euvoran bethought him that a single bird from the flock would still stand as the emblem and the talisman of his royalty in Ustaim, and would vindicate his quest among the isles of dawn. So, with a valiant hurling of sticks and stones, he tried to bring down one of the gazolbas. And ever before him as he chased them, the birds flew from tree to tree with a horrid shrieking, and a flurry of plumes that wrought an imperial splendor on the air. And at length, by his own good aim or the cast of chance, Euvoran slew him a gazolba.

As he went to retrieve the fallen bird, he saw a man in tattered raiment of an uncouth cut, armed with a rude bow, and carrying over his shoulder a brace of gazolbas tied together at the feet with tough grass. And the man

wore in lieu of other headgear the skin and feathers of the same fowl. He
came toward Euvoran, shouting indistinctly through his matted beard; and
the king beheld him with surprise and anger, and cried loudly:

"Vile serf, how darest thou to kill the bird that is sacred to the kings of
Ustaim? And knowest thou not that only the kings may wear the bird for
headgear? I, who am King Euvoran, shall hold thee to a dire accounting of
these deeds."

At this, eyeing Euvoran strangely, the man laughed a long and derisive laugh, as if he deemed the king a person somewhat addled in his wits.
And he seemed to find much merriment in the aspect of the king, whose
garments were draggled and were stiff and stained with the drying sea-
water, and whose turban had been snatched away by the felon waves,
leaving his baldness without disguise. And when he had done laughing, the
man said:

"Verily, this is the first and only jest that I have heard in nine years,
and my laughter must be forgiven. For nine years agone I was shipwrecked
on this isle, being a sea-captain from the far southwestern land of Ullotroi,
and the sole member of my ship's company that survived and came safe to
shore. In all those years I have held speech with no other man, since the isle
is remote from the maritime routes, and has no people other than the
birds. And as for your questions, they are readily answered: I kill these fowl
to avert the pangs of famine, since there is little else on the isle for sustenance, apart from roots and berries. And I wear on my head the skin and
feathers of the fowl because my tarboosh was stolen by the sea whenas it
flung me rudely upon this strand. And I wot not of the strange laws that
you mention; and moreover, your kingship is a matter that concerns me

little, since the isle is kingless, and you and I are alone thereon, and I am the stronger of us twain and the better armed. Therefore be well advised, O King Euvoran; and since you have slain yourself a bird, I counsel you to pick up the bird and come with me. Truly, it may be that I can help you in the matter of spitting and broiling this fowl: for I must deem that you are more familiar with the products of the culinary art than with the practice."

Now, hearing all this, the wrath of Euvoran sank within him like a flame that fails for oil. Clearly he saw the plight to which his voyage had brought him in the end; and bitterly he discerned the irony that was hidden in the true oracle of Geol. And he knew that the wreckage of his fleet of war was scattered among lost islands or blown into seas unvoyageable. And it came to him that never again should he see the marble houses of Aramoam, nor live in pleasant luxury, nor administer the dooms of law between the torturer and the executioner in the hall of justice, nor wear the gazolba-crown amid the plaudits of his people. So, not being utterly bereft of reason, he bowed him to his destiny.

And he said to the sea-captain, "There is sense in what you say. Therefore lead on."

Then, laden with the spoils of the chase, Euvoran and the captain, whose name was Naz Obbamar, repaired companionably to a cave in the rocky hill-slope of the isle's interior, which Naz Obbamar had chosen for his abode. Here the captain made a fire of dry cedar boughs, and showed the king the proper manner in which to pluck his fowl and broil it over the fire, turning it slowly on a spit of green camphor-wood. And Euvoran, being famished, found the meat of the gazolba far from unpalatable, though somewhat lean and strongly flavored. And after they had eaten,

Naz Obbamar brought out from the cave a rough jar of the island clay containing a wine he had made from certain berries; and he and Euvoran drank from the jar by turns, and told each other the tale of their adventures, and forgot for a while the rudeness and desolation of their plight.

Thereafter they shared the isle of gazolbas, killing and eating the birds as their hunger ordained. Sometimes, for a great delicacy, they slew and ate some other fowl that was more rarely met on the isle, though common enough, perhaps in Ustaim or Ullotroi. And King Euvoran made him a headdress from the skin and plumes of the gazolba, even as Naz Obbamar had done. And this was the fashion of their days till the end.

THE MAZE OF THE ENCHANTER

With no other light than that of the four diminutive moons of Xiccarph, each in a different phase but all decrescent, Tiglari had crossed the bottomless swamp of Soorm, wherein no reptile dwelt and no dragon descended—but where the pitch-black ooze was alive with continual heavings and writhings. He had carefully avoided the high causey of white corundum that spanned the fen, and had threaded his way with infinite peril from isle to sedgy isle that shuddered gelatinously beneath him. When he reached the solid shore and the shelter of the palm-tall rushes, he was equally careful to avoid the pale porphyry stairs that wound heavenward through dizzy, nadir-cleaving chasms and along glassy scarps to the ever-mysterious and terrible house of Maal Dweb. The causey and the stairs were guarded by those that he did not wish to meet: the silent, colossal iron servitors of Maal Dweb, whose arms ended in long crescent blades of tempered steel which were raised in implacable scything against any who came thither without their master's permission.

Tiglari's naked body was smeared from crown to heel with the juice of a jungle plant repugnant to all the fauna of Xiccarph. By virtue of this he hoped to pass unharmed the ferocious ape-like creatures that roamed at will through the cliff-hung gardens and halls of the Tyrant. He carried a coil of woven root-fiber, wonderfully strong and light, and weighted with a brazen ball at one end, for use in climbing the mountain. At his side, in a sheath of chimera-skin, he wore a needle-sharp knife that had been dipt in the mortal poison of winged vipers.

Many, before Tiglari, with the same noble dream of tyrannicide, had attempted to cross the pitchy fen and scale the forbidding scarps. But none had returned; and the fate of such as had actually won to the mountain palace of Maal Dweb was a much-disputed problem; since no man had ever again beheld them, living or dead. But Tiglari, the jungle hunter, skilled in the slaying of fierce and crafty beasts, was undeterred by the more than hideous probabilities before him.

The escalade of the mountain would have been a highly dangerous feat by the full light of the three suns of Xiccarph. With eyes that were keen as those of some night-flying pterodactyl, Tiglari hurled his weighted coil about projecting coigns and fang-like salients. Hand over hand, he went up with simian ease from foothold to precarious foothold; and at length he attained a narrow buttress beneath the final cliff. From this vantage, it was an easy matter to fling his rope around the crooked bole of a tree that leaned gulfward with scimitar-like foliage from the gardens of Maal Dweb.

Evading the sharp and semi-metallic leaves that seemed to slash downward as the tree bent limberly with his dangling weight, he stood, stooping warily, on the fearsome and widely fabled mesa. Here, it was rumored, with no human aid, the half-demoniac sorcerer and scientist had carved the more lofty pinnacles of the old mountain into walls, cupolas and turrets, and had levelled a great space about them. This space he had covered immediately with loamy soil, produced by magic; and therein he had planted curious baneful trees from outlying worlds beyond the suns of Xiccarph, together with flowers that might have been those of some teeming and exuberant hell.

Little enough was actually known of these gardens; but the flora that grew on the northern, southern and western sides of the palace was popularly believed to be less deadly than that which faced the dawning of the triple suns. Much of this latter vegetation, according to myth, had been trained and topiarized in the form of an almost infinite labyrinth, balefully ingenious, from which egress was impossible: a maze that concealed in its windings the most fatal and atrocious traps, the most unpredictable dooms, invented by the malign Daedalus. Mindful of this labyrinth, Tiglari had approached the place on the side that fronted the three-fold sunset.

Breathless, with arms that ached from the long, arduous climb, he crouched in the garden shadows. About him he saw the heavy-hooded blossoms that leaned from a winy gloom in venomous languour, or fawned toward him with open corollas that exhaled a narcotic perfume or diffused a pollen of madness. Anomalous, multiform, with silhouettes that curdled the blood or touched the brain with nightmare, the trees of Maal Dweb appeared to gather and conspire against him beyond the flowers. Some arose with the sinuous towering of plumed pythons, or aigretted dragons. Others crouched with radiating limbs that were like the hairy members of colossal arachnidans. They seemed to close in upon Tiglari with a stealthy motion. They waved their frightful darts of thorn, their scythe-like leaves. They blotted the four moons with webs of arabesque menace. They reared from interminably coiling roots behind mammoth foliages that resembled an army of interlocking shields.

With endless caution and calculation, the hunter made his way forward, seeking a rift in the armed phalanx of vegetable monstrosities. His faculties, ever alert, were abnormally quickened by a grievous fear, intensified by a mighty hatred. The fear was not for himself, but for the girl Athlé, his beloved and the fairest of his tribe, who had gone up alone that very evening by the causey of corundum and the porphyry stairs at the summons of Maal Dweb. His hatred was that of a brave man and an outraged lover for the all-powerful, all-dreaded tyrant whom no man had ever seen, and from whose abode no woman came back; who spoke with an iron voice that was audible at will in the far cities or the outmost jungles; who punished the rebellious and the disobedient with a doom of falling fire that was swifter than the thunderstone.

Maal Dweb had taken ever the fairest from among the maidens of the planet Xiccarph; and no palace of the walled towns, or savage outland cave, was exempt from his unknown scrutiny. He had chosen no less than fifty girls during the three decades of his tyranny; and these, forsaking their lovers and kinsfolk voluntarily, lest the wrath of Maal Dweb should descend upon them, had gone one by one to the mountain citadel and were lost behind its cryptic walls. There, as the odalisques of the aging sorcerer, they were supposed to dwell in halls that multiplied their beauty with a thousand mirrors; and were said to have for servants women of brass and men of iron that mimicked in all ways the motion and speech of living people.

Tiglari had poured before Athlé the uncouth adoration of his heart and the barbaric spoils of the chase, but having many rivals, was still unsure of her favor. Cool as a river lily, and no less impartial, she had accepted his worship and that of the others, among whom the warrior Mocair was perhaps the most formidable. Returning at eve from the hunt, Tiglari had found the tribe in lamentation; and, learning that Athlé had departed to the harem of Maal Dweb, was swift to follow.

He had not announced his intention to his fellow tribesmen, since the ears of Maal Dweb were everywhere; and he did not know whether Mocair or any of the others had preceded him in his desperate errantry. Mocair, however, had been absent; and it was not unlikely that he had already dared the obscure and hideous perils of the mountain.

The thought of this was enough to drive Tiglari forward with a rash disregard of the poisonous, reptile flowers and clutching foliations. He came anon to a gap in the horrible grove, and saw the saffron lights from the lower windows of Maal Dweb, and a dark thronging of domes and turrets that assailed the constellations above. The lights were vigilant as the eyes of sleepless dragons, and appeared to regard him with an evil, unblinking awareness. But Tiglari leapt toward them, across the gap, and heard the clash of sabered leaves that met behind him.

Before him was an open lawn, covered with a queer grass that squirmed like innumerable worms beneath his bare feet. He did not care to linger upon that lawn, but ran onward with light, skimming paces. There were no footmarks in the grass; but nearing the portico of the palace, he saw a coil of thin rope that someone had flung aside, and knew that Mocair had preceded him.

There were paths of mottled marble about the palace, and fountains and waterfalls that played with a gurgling as of blood from the throats of carven monsters. The open portals were unguarded, and the whole building was still as a mausoleum lit by windless lamps. No shadows moved behind the brilliant yellow windows; and darkness slept unbroken among the high towers and cupolas. Tiglari, however, mistrusted sorely the appearance of quietude and slumber, and followed the bordering paths for some distance before daring to approach nearer to the palace.

Certain large and shadowy animals, which he took for the apish monsters of Maal Dweb, went by him in the gloom. They were hairy and uncouth, with sloping heads. Some of them ran in four-footed fashion, while others maintained the half-erect posture of anthropoids. They did not offer to molest Tiglari; but, whining dismally like dogs, they slunk away as if to avoid him. By this token, he knew that they were veritable beasts, and could not abide the odor with which he had smeared his limbs and torso.

At length, he came to a lampless portico with crowded columns. Here, with the silent gliding of a jungle snake, he entered the mysterious and ever-dreadful house of Maal Dweb. Behind the dark pillars, a door stood open; and beyond the door were the dim and seemingly endless reaches of an empty hall.

Tiglari went in with redoubled caution, and began to follow the arrased wall. The place was full of unknown perfumes, languorous and somnolent: a subtle reek as of censers in hidden alcoves of love. He did not like the perfumes; and the silence troubled him more and more as he went deeper into the palace. It seemed to him that the darkness was thick with unheard breathings, was alive with invisible and sinister movements.

Slowly, like the opening of great yellow eyes, the yellow flames arose in mighty lamps of copper that hung along the hall. Tiglari hid himself behind a heavy-figured arras; but peeping out with eerie trepidation, he saw that the hall was still deserted. Finally, he dared to resume his progress. All about him, the imperial hangings, broidered with purple men and azure women on a field of bright blood, appeared to stir with easy life in a wind that he could not feel; and the lamps regarded him with unwavering splendid eyes. But there was no sign of the presence of Maal Dweb; and the metal servitors and human odalisques of the tyrant were nowhere to be seen.

The doors on either side of the hall, with cunningly mated valves of ebony and ivory, were all closed. At the far end, Tiglari saw a rift of flaming light in a somber double arras. Parting the arras very softly, he peered into a huge, brightly illumined chamber that seemed at first sight to be the harem of Maal Dweb, peopled with all the girls that the enchanter had summoned to his mountain dwelling over a course of decades. In fact, it seemed that there were many hundreds, leaning or recumbent on ornate couches, or standing in attitudes of languor or terror. Tiglari discerned in the throng the women of Ommu-Zain, whose flesh is whiter than desert salt; the slim girls of Uthmai, who are moulded from breathing, palpitating jet; the queenly amber girls of equatorial Xala; and the small women of Ilap, who have the tones of newly greening bronze. But among them all, he could not find the lilied beauty of Athlé.

Greatly did he marvel at the number of the women and the utter stillness with which they maintained their various postures. There was no lifting nor falling of eyelids, no dropping of hands, no curving nor opening of lips. They were like images of living, subtly painted marble, or goddesses that slept in some enchanted hall of eternity.

Tiglari, the intrepid hunter, was awed and frightened. Here, surely, was proof of the fabled sorceries of Maal Dweb. These women—if indeed they were women and not mere statues—had been made the thralls of a death-like spell of immortal slumber. It was as if some invisible medium of adamantine silence had filled the room, had formed about its occupants: a silence wherein, it seemed, no mortal being could draw breath.

However, if Tiglari were to continue his search for Maal Dweb and Athlé, it was necessary for him to traverse the enchanted chamber. Feeling that a marble sleep might descend upon him at the very crossing of the sill, he went with holden breath and furtive pard-like paces. About him, the women preserved their eternal stillness, their various airs and attitudes. Each, it appeared, had been overcome by the spell at the instant of some particular emotion, whether of fear, wonder, curiosity, vanity, weariness, anger or voluptuousness. Their number was fewer than he had supposed, and the room itself was smaller, but metal mirrors, panelling the walls, had created an illusion of multitude and immensity.

At the further end, he came to a second double arras, slightly parted, and revealing only shadow beyond. Peering through, he beheld a twilight chamber, illuminated dimly by two censers that gave forth a parti-colored glow and a red fume as of vaporing blood. The censers were set on lofty tripods in the far corners, facing each other. Between them, beneath a canopy of some dark and smouldering stuff with fringes braided like women's hair, was a couch of nocturnal purples with a valance of silver birds that fought against golden snakes. On the couch, in sober garments, a man reclined as if weary or asleep. The face of the man was a pale mask of mystery lying amid ambiguous shadows; but it did not occur to Tiglari that this being was any other than the redoubtable and tyrannic sorcerer whom he had come to slay. He knew that this was Maal Dweb, whom no man had seen in the flesh, but whose power was manifest to all; the occult, omniscient ruler of Xiccarph; the overlord of kings; the suzerain of the three suns and of all their moons and planets.

Like ghostly sentinels, the symbols of the grandeur of Maal Dweb, the images of his frightful empire, rose up to confront Tiglari. But the thought of Athlé was a red mist that blotted all. He forgot his eerie terrors, his awe of the ensorcelled palace. The rage of the bereaved lover, the bloodthirst of the cunning hunter, awoke within him to guide his agile, stealthy paces, to make firm his powerful thews. The chamber was empty, except for the still and languid figure on the couch. Tiglari neared the unconscious sorcerer; and his hand grew tight on the hilt of the needle-like knife that was dipt in viper-venom.

The man before him lay with closed eyes and a cryptic weariness on his mouth and eyelids. He seemed to meditate rather than sleep, like one who wanders in a maze of distant memories or profound reveries. About him the walls were draped with funereal hangings, darkly and vaguely figured. Above him the twin censers wrought a cloudy glow, and diffused throughout the room their drowsy myrrh, which made the senses of Tiglari swim with a strange dimness.

Crouching tiger-wise beside the valance of birds and serpents, he made ready for the stroke. Then, mastering the subtle vertigo of the perfumes, he rose up; and his arm, with the darting movement of some heavy but supple adder, struck fiercely at the tyrant's heart.

It was as if he had tried to pierce a wall of adamant. In mid-air, before and above the recumbent enchanter, the knife clashed on some impenetrable substance that Tiglari could not see; and the point broke off and tinkled on the floor at his feet. Uncomprehending, baffled, he peered at the being whom he had sought to slay. Maal Dweb had not stirred nor opened his eyes. There was neither frown nor smile on his features; but their look of enigmatic weariness was somehow touched with a faint and cruel amusement.

Hesitantly, Tiglari put out his hand to verify a certain curious notion that had occurred to him. Even as he had suspected, there was no couch or canopy between the fuming censers—only a vertical, unbroken, highly-polished surface, in which the whole scene was apparently reflected. He had tried to kill a mirrored image. But, to his further mystification, he himself was not visible in the mirror.

He whirled about, thinking Maal Dweb must be somewhere in the room. Even as he turned, the funereal draperies rushed back with an evil, silken whispering from the wall, as if drawn by unseen hands. The chamber leaped into sudden glaring light, the walls appeared to recede illimitably; and naked giants, whose umber-brown limbs and torsos glistened as if smeared with ointment, stood in menacing postures on every side. Their eyes glowered like those of jungle creatures; and each of them held an enormous knife, from which the point had been broken.

This, thought Tiglari, was a fearsome thaumaturgy; and he crouched down beneath the tripods, wary as a trapped animal, to await the assault of the giants. But these beings, crouching simultaneously, mimicked his every movement. By degrees it came to him that what he saw was his own reflection, multiplied and monstrously amplified in the mirrors of Maal Dweb.

He turned again. The tasseled canopy, the couch of night-dark purples with its figured valance, the reclining dreamer in plain vestments, all had vanished. Of that which he had beheld, only the smoking censers remained, rearing before a glassy wall that gave back like the others the reflection of Tiglari himself.

Bafflement and terror united now in the savage brain of the hunter. He felt that Maal Dweb, the all-seeing, all-potent magician, was playing a game and was deluding him with elaborate mockeries. Rashly indeed had Tiglari pitted his simple brawn and forest craft against a being of such supernatural power and demoniac artifice. He dared not stir; he scarcely ventured to breathe. The monstrous reflections appeared to watch him like ogres who guard a captive pygmy. The light, which emanated as if from hidden lamps in the mirrors, took on a more pitiless and alarming luster, and centered itself upon him with a silent horror. The vast, illusive reaches of the room appeared to deepen; and far away in their shadows, he saw the gathering of vapors with human faces that melted and re-formed incessantly and were never twice the same.

Ever the eerie radiance brightened; ever the mist of faces, like a hell-born fume, dissolved and re-limned itself behind the immobile giants, in the lengthening vistas. An unheard laughter, malevolent, scornful, seemed to lurk beyond the stillness. How long Tiglari waited, he could not tell; the bright and frozen horror of that room was a thing apart from time.

Now, in the litten air, a voice began to speak; a voice that was toneless, deliberate—and disembodied. It was faintly contemptuous; a little weary;

slightly cruel. It was impossible to align or locate; near as the beating of Tiglari's heart, and yet infinitely far.

"What do you seek, Tiglari?" said the voice. "Do you think to enter with impunity the palace of Maal Dweb? Others—many others, with the same intentionshave come before you: but all have paid a certain price for their temerity."

"I seek the maiden Athlé," said Tiglari. "What have you done with her?" The words were strange to him, their very sound was remote, as if another than himself had spoken.

"Athlé is very beautiful," replied the voice. "It is the will of Maal Dweb to make a certain use of her loveliness. The use is not one that should concern a hunter of wild beasts . . . You are unwise, Tiglari."

"Where is Athlé?" persisted the hunter.

"Athlé has gone to find her fate in the labyrinth of Maal Dweb. Not long ago, the warrior Mocair, who had followed her to my palace, went out at my suggestion to pursue his search amid the threadless windings of that never to be exhausted maze. Go now, Tiglari, and seek her also . . . There are many mysteries in my labyrinth; and among them all, mayhap, there is one which you are destined to solve."

The hunter saw that a door had opened in the mirror-panelled wall. In the depth of the mirrors, two of the metal slaves of Maal Dweb had appeared. Taller than living men, and gleaming from head to foot with implacable lusters as of burnished swords, they came forward upon Tiglari. The right arm of each was handed with a crescent sickle. Hastily, with no backward glance, the hunter went out through the open door. Behind him he heard the surly clash of its meeting valves.

The short night of the planet Xiccarph was not yet over, and the four moons had all gone down. But before him he saw the beginning of the fabled maze, illuminated clearly by glowing globular fruits that hung lantern-wise from baroque arches and arcades of foliage. Guided by their still, uncanny luminescence, he entered the labyrinth.

At first, it was a place of elfin fantasies and whims. There were quaintly turned estrades, pillared with slim and antic trees, latticed with the drolly peering faces of extravagant orchids, that led the seeker to hidden, surprising bowers of goblinry. It was as if those outer meanderings had been planned merely to entice and bemuse and beguile.

Then, by vague degrees, as the hunter went on, it seemed that the designer's mood had darkened, had become more ominous and baleful. The trees that lined the path, with twisted, intertwining boles, were Laocoons of struggle and torture, lit by enormous fungi that seemed to lift unholy tapers. The path itself ran downward, or climbed with evilly tilted steps through caverns of imbricated leafage that shone with the brazen glistening of dragon-scales. At every turning the way divided before Tiglari; the devious branchings multiplied; and skillful though he was in jungle-craft, it would have been wholly impossible for him to retrace his wanderings. He kept on, hoping that chance would somehow lead him to Athlé; and many times he called her name aloud, but was answered only by remote, derisive echoes, or by the dolorous howling of some unseen beast that had become lost in the maze of Maal Dweb.

He came to eerie pools, alight with coiling and wreathing witch-fires, in dim arboreal grottoes. Greenish, bloated hands as of dead men appeared to lift from the changing films of phosphorescence; and once he thought that he beheld the drowning face of Athlé. He plunged into the shallow pool—but found only fetid slime, and a swollen, nauseous thing that squirmed slowly beneath his touch.

Now he was mounting through arbors of malignant hydra growths that coiled and uncoiled about him tumultuously. The way lightened more and more; the night-shining fruits and blossoms were pale and sickly as the dying tapers of a witches' revel. The earliest of the three suns had risen; and its gamboge-yellow beams were filtering in through the plaited horrors of frilled and venomous vines.

Far off, and seeming to fall from some hidden height in the labyrinth before him, he heard a chorus of brazen voices that were like articulate bells or gongs. He could not distinguish the words; but the accents were those of a solemn and portentous announcement. They were fraught with mystic finality, with hieratic doom. They ceased; and there was no sound other than the hiss and rustle of swaying plants.

Tiglari went on. The tortuous maze became wilder and more anomalous. There were tiered growths, like obscene sculptures or architectural forms, that seemed to be of stone and metal. Others were like carnal nightmares of rooted flesh, that wallowed and fought and coupled in noisome ooze. Foul things with chancrous blossoms flaunted themselves on infernal obelisks. Living parasitic mosses of crimson crawled on vegetable monsters that swelled and bloated behind the columns of accursed pavilions.

It seemed now that the hunter's every step was predestined and dictated. He was no longer free to choose his way; for many paths were overgrown by things that he did care to face; and others were blocked by horrid portcullises of cacti, or ended in pools whose waters teemed with leeches larger than tunnies. The second and third suns of Xiccarph arose; but their beams of emerald and carmine served but to heighten the terrors of the web that had closed in about Tiglari.

By stairs where floral serpents crept, and gradients lined with tossing, clashing aloes, he climbed slowly on. Rarely could he see the labyrinthine reaches below, or the levels toward which he was tending. Somewhere on the blind path, he met one of the ape-like animals of Maal Dweb: a dark, savage creature, sleek and glistening like a wet otter, as if it had bathed in one of the hidden pools. It passed him with a hoarse growl, recoiling as the others had done from his repulsively smeared body . . . But nowhere could he find the maiden Athlé or the warrior Mocair, who had preceded him into the maze.

Now he had reached a curious little pavement of somber onyx, oblong, and wholly surrounded, except on the side of his approach, by enormous flowers with fluted bronze-like stems and great leaning balls that seemed to be the mottled heads of bestial chimeras, yawning to disclose their carmine throats. Through the gap in this singular hedge, he stepped forward on the pavement and stood staring irresolutely at the serried blooms: for here the way seemed to end.

The onyx beneath his feet was wet with some unknown, sticky fluid. He was dazed with the wonder, strangeness, and intricate, coiling horror through which he had passed; but a dim warning of peril stirred within him. He turned toward the gap through which he had entered, but his impulse of retreat was all too late. From the base of each of the tall flower stems, a long tendril like a wire of bronze uncoiled with lightning rapidity, and closed about his ankles. He stood trapped and helpless at the center of a taut net. Then, while he struggled ineffectually, the huge stems began to lean and tilt toward him, till the carmine mouths of the blossoms were close about his knees like a circle of fawning monsters.

Nearer they came, almost touching him. From their thick lips a clear, hueless liquid, dripping slowly at first, and then running in little rills, descended on his feet and ankles and shanks. Indescribably, his flesh crawled beneath it; then there was a peculiar passing numbness; then a furious stinging like the bites of innumerable insects. Between the crowding heads of the flowers he saw that his legs had undergone a mysterious and horrifying change; their natural hairiness had thickened, had assumed a dark and shaggy pile like the fur of apes; the shanks themselves had somehow shortened; and the feet had grown longer, with uncouth finger-like toes such as were possessed by the animals of Maal Dweb!

In a frenzy of nameless alarm and fear, he drew his broken-tipped knife and began to slash at the flowers. It was as if he had struck at monstrous bells of ringing iron, had assailed the armored heads of dragons. The blade snapped at the hilt. Then the blossoms, lifting hideously, were leaning about his waist, were laving his hips and thighs in their thin, evil slaver.

Across the bizarre nightmare in which his brain and body were drowning impotently, he heard the startled cry of a woman. Through the open gap in the hedge, he beheld a strange scene which the hitherto impenetrable maze, parting as if magic, had revealed. Fifty feet away, on the same level as the onyx pavement, there stood an elliptic dais or low altar of moonwhite stone at whose center the maiden Athlé, emerging from the labyrinth on a raised walk of porphyry, had paused in an attitude of wonder. Before her, in the claws of an immense marble lizard that reared above the dais, a great circular mirror of steely metal was held upright, with the monster's head hidden from view behind it. Athle', as if fascinated by some celestial vision, was peering into the steely disk. She presented her wide-eyed profile to Tiglari; and the mirror itself was seen obliquely, with the foreshortened body of the lizard reaching away at a sharp angle and mingling obscenely with the half-reptilian maze. Midway between the onyx pavement and the ellipse of pale stone, a row of six slender brazen columns, topped with graven heads like demoniac Termini, rose at broad intervals and faced alternately the hunter and the girl.

Tiglari would have called out to Athlé; but at that moment she took a single step toward the mirror, as if drawn by something that she saw in its depths; and the dull disk seemed to brighten with some internal, incandescent flame. The eyes of the hunter were temporarily blinded by the spiky rays that leapt forth from it for an instant, enveloping and transfixing the maiden. When the dimness cleared away in swirling blots of sultry color, he saw that Athlé, in a pose of statuesque rigidity, was still regarding the mirror with startled eyes. She had not moved; the wonder was frozen on her face: and it came to Tiglari that she was like the women who slept an enchanted slumber in the palace of Maal Dweb. Even as this thought occurred to him, he heard the ringing chorus of metallic voices, that seemed to emanate from the graven demon heads upon the columns.

"The maiden Athlé," announced the voices in solemn and portentous tones, "has beheld herself in the mirror of Eternity, and has passed forever beyond the changes and corruptions of Time."

Tiglari felt that he was sinking into some enormous, obscurely terrible fen of dreams. He could comprehend nothing of what had befallen Athlé; and his own fate was an equally dark and dread enigma beyond the solution of a simple hunter.

Now the leaning blossoms had lifted about his shoulders, were laving his arms, his body. Beneath their abhorrent alchemy the transformation continued. A long fur sprang up on the thickening torso; the arms lengthened; they became simian; the hands took on a likeness to the feet. From the neck downward, Tiglari differed in no wise from the apes of the garden.

In helpless abject terror, he waited for the completion of the metamorphosis. Then, slowly, he became aware that a man in sober garments, with eyes and mouth replete with the weariness of strange things, was standing before him. Behind the man, as if attending him, were two of the sickle-handed automatons of iron.

In a somewhat languid voice, the man uttered an unknown word that vibrated in the air with prolonged, mysterious aftertones. The circle of craning flowers drew back from Tiglari, resuming their former upright positions in a weird hedge; and the wiry tendrils were withdrawn from his ankles, leaving him free. Hardly able to comprehend his release, he heard a sound of brazen voices, and knew dimly that the demon heads of the columns had spoken, saying:

"The hunter Tiglari has been laved in the nectar of the blossoms of primordial life, and has become in all ways, from the neck downward, even as the beasts that he hunted."

When the solemn chorus ceased, the weary man in sober raiment came nearer and addressed him:

"I, Maal Dweb, had intended to deal with you precisely as I dealt with Mocair and many others. Mocair was the beast that you met in the labyrinth, with new-made fur that was still sleek and wet from the liquor of the flowers; and you saw some of his predecessors about the palace. However, I find that my whims are not always the same. You, Tiglari, unlike the others, shall at least remain a man from the neck upward; and you are free to resume your wanderings in the labyrinth, and escape from it if you can. I do not wish to see you again, and my clemency arises from another reason than esteem for your kind. Go now: the maze has many windings which you are yet to traverse."

A dreadful awe was upon Tiglari; his native fierceness, his savage volition, were tamed by the enchanter's languid will. With one backward look of fearful concern and wonder at the frozen shape of Athlé, he withdrew obediently, slouching like a great ape. His fur glistening wetly to the three suns, he vanished amid the meanderings of the labyrinth.

Maal Dweb, attended by his metal slaves, went over to the figure of Athlé, which still regarded the steely mirror with astonished eyes.

"Mong Lut," he said, addressing by name the nearer of the two automatons that followed at his heels, "it has been, as you know, my caprice to eternalize the frail beauty of women. Athlé, like the others whom I have summoned to the mountain and have sent out to explore the ingenious maze, has looked upon that mirror whose sudden radiance turns the flesh to a stone that is fairer than marble and no less eternal . . . Also, as you know, it has been my whim to turn men into beasts with the copious fluid of certain artificial flowers, so that their outer semblance should conform strictly to their inner nature. Is it not well, Mong Lut, that I should have done these things? Am I not Maal Dweb, in whom all knowledge and all power reside?"

"Yes, master," echoed the automaton in an iron voice, "you are Maal Dweb, the all-wise, the all-powerful, and it is well that you should have done these things."

"However," continued Maal Dweb, "the repetition of even the most remarkable thaumaturgies can grow monotonous after a certain number of times. I do not think that I shall deal again in this fashion with any woman, nor deal thus with any man. Is it not well, Mong Lut, that I should vary my sorceries in future? Am I not Maal Dweb, the all-resourceful?"

"Indeed, you are Maal Dweb," agreed the automaton, "and it would be well for you to diversify your enchantments."

Maal Dweb, in his manner, was not ill pleased with the answers that the automaton had given. He cared little for converse, other than the iron echoing of his metal servitors, who assented always to all that he said, and who spared him the tedium of arguments. And it may have been that there were times when he wearied a little even of this, and preferred the silence of the petrified women, or the muteness of the beasts that could no longer call themselves men.

THE DOUBLE SHADOW

My name is Pharpetron, among those who have known me in Poseidonis; but even I, the last and most forward pupil of the wise Avyctes, know not the name of that which I am fated to become ere tomorrow. Therefore, by the ebbing silver lamps, in my master's marble house above the loud, ever-ravening sea, I write this tale with a hasty hand, scrawling an ink of wizard virtue on the grey, priceless, antique parchment of dragons. And having written, I shall enclose the pages in a sealed cylinder of orichalchum, and shall cast the cylinder from a high window into the sea, lest that which I am doomed to become should haply destroy the writing. And it may be that mariners from Lephara, passing to Umb and Pneor in their tall triremes, will find the cylinder; or fishers will draw it from the wave in their seines of byssus; and having read my story, men will learn the truth and take warning; and no man's feet, henceforward, will approach the pale and demon-haunted house of Avyctes.

For six years, I have dwelt apart with the aged master, forgetting youth and its wonted desires in the study of arcanic things. Together, we have delved more deeply than all others before us in an interdicted lore; we have solved the keyless hieroglyphs that guard ante-human formulae; we have talked with the prehistoric dead; we have called up the dwellers in sealed crypts, in fearful abysses beyond space. Few are the sons of mankind who have cared to seek us out among the desolate, wind-worn crags; and many, but nameless, are the visitants who have come to us from further bourns of place and time.

Stern and white as a tomb, older than the memory of the dead, and built by men or devils beyond the recording of myth, is the mansion in which we dwell. Far below, on black, naked reefs, the northern sea climbs and roars indomitably, or ebbs with a ceaseless murmur as of armies of baffled demons; and the house is filled evermore, like a hollow-sounding sepulcher, with the drear echo of its tumultuous voices; and the winds wail in dismal wrath around the high towers, but shake them not. On the seaward side, the mansion rises sheerly from the straight-falling cliff; but on the other sides there are narrow terraces, grown with dwarfish, crooked cedars that bow always beneath the gale. Giant marble monsters guard the landward portals; and huge marble women ward the strait porticoes above the sea; and mighty statues and mummies stand everywhere in the chambers and along the halls. But, saving these, and the spirits we have summoned, there is none to companion us; and liches and shadows have been the servitors of our daily needs.

All men have heard the fame of Avyctes, the sole surviving pupil of that Malygris who tyrannized in his necromancy over Susran from a tower of sable stone; Malygris, who lay dead for years while men believed him living; who, lying thus, still uttered potent spells and dire oracles with decaying lips. But Avyctes lusted not for temporal power in the manner of Malygris; and having learned all that the elder sorcerer could teach him, withdrew from the cities of Poseidonis to seek another and vaster dominion; and I, the youth Pharpetron, in the latter years of Avyctes, was permitted to join him in this solitude; and since then, I have shared his austerities and vigils and evocations . . . and now, likewise, I must share the weird doom that has come in answer to his summoning.

Not without terror (since man is but mortal) did I, the neophyte, behold at first the abhorrent and tremendous faces of them that obeyed Avyctes: the genii of the sea and earth, of the stars and the heavens, who passed to and fro in his marmorean halls. I shuddered at the black writhing of submundane things from the many-volumed smoke of the braziers; I cried in horror at the grey foulnesses, colossal, without form, that crowded malignly about the drawn circle of seven colors, threatening unspeakable trespass on us that stood at the center. Not without revulsion did I drink wine that was poured by cadavers, and eat bread that was purveyed by phantoms. But use and custom dulled the strangeness, destroyed the fear; and in time I believed implicitly that Avyctes was the lord of all incantations and exorcisms, with infallible power to dismiss the beings he evoked.

Well had it had been for Avyctes—and for me—if the master had contented himself with the lore preserved from Atlantis and Thule, or brought over from Mu and Mayapan. Surely this should have been enough: for in the ivory-sheeted books of Thule there were blood-writ runes that would call the demons of the fifth and seventh planets, if spoken aloud at the hour of their ascent; and the sorcerers of Mu had left record of a process whereby the doors of far-future time could be unlocked; and our fathers, the Atlanteans, had known the road between the atoms and the path into far stars, and had held speech with the spirits of the sun. But Avyctes thirsted for a darker knowledge, a deeper empery; and into his hands, in the third year of my novitiate, there came the mirror-bright tablet of the lost serpent-people.

Strange, and apparently fortuitous, was our finding of the tablet. At certain hours, when the tide had fallen from the steep rocks, we were wont to descend by cavern-hidden stairs to a cliff-walled crescent beach behind the promontory on which stood the house of Avyctes. There, on the dun, wet sands, beyond the foamy tongues of the surf, would lie the worn and curious driftage of alien shores, and trove that hurricanes had cast up from unsounded deeps. And there we had found the purple and sanguine volutes of great shells, and rude lumps of ambergris, and white flowers of perpetually blooming coral; and once, the barbaric idol of green brass that had been the figurehead of a galley from far hyperboreal isles.

There had been a great storm, such as must have riven the sea to its nethermost profound; but the tempest had gone by with morning, and the heavens were cloudless on that fatal day when we found the tablet, and the demon winds were hushed among the high crags and chasms; and the sea lisped with a low whisper, like the rustle of gowns of samite trailed by fleeing maidens on the sand. And just beyond the ebbing wave, in a tangle of russet seaweed, we beheld a thing that glittered with blinding sun-like brilliance. And running forward, I plucked it from the wrack before the wave's return, and bore it to Avyctes.

The tablet was wrought of some nameless metal, like never-rusting iron, but heavier. It had the form of a triangle and was broader at the widest than a man's heart. On one side it was wholly blank; and Avyctes and I, in turn, beheld our features mirrored strangely, like the drawn, pallid features of the dead, in its burnished surface. On the other side many rows of small crooked ciphers were incised deeply in the metal, as if by the action of some mordant acid; and these ciphers were not the pictorial symbols or alphabetic characters of any language known to the master or to me.

Of the tablet's age and origin, likewise, we could form no conjecture; and our erudition was altogether baffled. For many days thereafter we studied the writing and held argument that came to no issue. And night by night, in a high chamber closed against the perennial winds, we pondered over the dazzling triangle by the tall straight flames of silver lamps. For Avyctes deemed that knowledge of rare value (or haply some secret of an alien or elder magic) was holden by the clueless crooked ciphers. Then, since all our scholarship was in vain, the master sought another divination, and had recourse to wizardy and necromancy. But at first, among the devils and phantoms that answered our interrogation, none could tell us aught concerning the tablet. And any other than Avyctes would have despaired in the end . . . and well would it have been if he had despaired, and had sought no longer to decipher the writing. . . .

The months and years went by with a slow thundering of seas on the dark rocks, and a headlong clamor of winds around the white towers. Still we continued our delvings and evocations; and further, always further we went into lampless realms of space and spirit; learning, perchance, to unlock the hithermost of the manifold infinities. And at whiles, Avyctes would resume his pondering of the sea-found tablet; or would question some visitant from other spheres of time and place regarding its interpretation.

At last, by the use of a chance formula, in idle experiment, he summoned up the dim, tenuous ghost of a sorcerer from prehistoric years;

and the ghost, in a thin whisper of uncouth, forgotten speech, informed us that the letters on the tablet were those of a language of the serpent-men, whose primordial continent had sunk aeons before the lifting of Hyperborea from the ooze. But the ghost could tell us naught of their significance; for, even in his time, the serpent-people had become a dubious legend; and their deep, ante-human lore and sorcery were things irretrievable by man.

Now, in all the books of conjuration owned by Avyctes, there was no spell whereby we could call the lost serpent-men from their fabulous epoch. But there was an old Lemurian formula, recondite and uncertain, by which the shadow of a dead man could be sent into years posterior to those of his own life-time, and could be recalled after an interim by the wizard. And the shade, being wholly insubstantial, would suffer no harm from the temporal transition, and would remember, for the information of the wizard, that which he had been instructed to learn during the journey.

So, having called again the ghost of the prehistoric sorcerer, whose name was Ybith, Avyctes made a singular use of several very ardent gums and combustible fragments of fossil wood; and he and I, reciting the responses to the formula, sent the thin spirit of Ybith into the far ages of the serpent-men. And after a time which the master deemed sufficient, we performed the curious rites of incantation that would recall Ybith from his alienage. And the rites were successful; and Ybith stood before us again, like a blown vapor that is nigh to vanishing. And in words that were faint as the last echo of perishing memories, the specter told us the key to the meaning of the letters, which he had learned in the primeval past; and after this, we questioned Ybith no more, but suffered him to return unto slumber and oblivion.

Then, knowing the import of the tiny, twisted ciphers, we read the writing on the tablet and made thereof a transliteration, though not without labor and difficulty, since the very phonetics of the serpent tongue, and the symbols and ideas expressed in the writing, were somewhat alien to those of mankind. And when we had mastered the inscription, we found that it contained the formula for a certain evocation which, no doubt, had been used by the serpent sorcerers. But the object of the evocation was not named; nor was there any clue to the nature or identity of that which would come in answer to the rites. And moreover there was no corresponding rite of exorcism nor spell of dismissal.

Great was the jubilation of Avyctes, deeming that we had learned a lore beyond the memory or prevision of man. And though I sought to dissuade him, he resolved to employ the evocation, arguing that our discovery was no chance thing but was fatefully predestined from the beginning. And he seemed to think lightly of the menace that might be brought upon us by the conjuration of things whose nativity and attributes were wholly obscure. "For," said Avyctes, "I have called up, in all the years of my sorcery, no god or devil, no demon or lich or shadow, which I could not control and dismiss at will. And I am loath to believe that any power or spirit beyond the subversion of my spells could have been summoned by a race of serpents, whatever their skill in demonism and necromancy."

So, seeing that he was obstinate, and acknowledging him for my master in all ways, I consented to aid Avyctes in the experiment, though not without dire misgivings. And then we gathered together, in the chamber of conjuration, at the specified hour and configuration of the stars, the equivalents of sundry rare materials that the tablet had instructed us to use in the ritual.

Of much that we did, and of certain agents that we employed, it were better not to tell; nor shall I record the shrill, sibilant words, difficult for beings not born of serpents to articulate, whose intonation formed a signal part of the ceremony. Toward the last, we drew a triangle on the marble floor with the fresh blood of birds; and Avyctes stood at one angle, and I at another; and the gaunt umber mummy of an Atlantean warrior, whose name had been Oigos, was stationed at the third angle. And standing thus, Avyctes and I held tapers of corpse-tallow in our hands, till the tapers had burned down between our fingers as into a socket. And in the outstretched palms of the mummy of Oigos, as if in shallow thuribles, talc and asbestos burned, ignited by a strange fire whereof we knew the secret. At one side we had traced on the floor an infrangible ellipse, made by an endless linked repetition of the twelve unspeakable Signs of Oumor, to which we could retire if the visitant should prove inimical or rebellious. We waited while the pole-circling stars went over, as had been prescribed. Then, when the tapers had gone out between our seared fingers, and the talc and asbestos were wholly consumed in the mummy's eaten palms, Avyctes uttered a single word whose sense was obscure to us; and Oigos, being animated by sorcery and subject to our will, repeated the word after a given interval, in tones that were hollow as a tomb-born echo; and I in my turn also repeated it.

Now, in the chamber of evocation, before beginning the ritual, we had opened a small window giving upon the sea, and had likewise left open a high door on the hall to landward, lest that which came in answer to us should require a spatial mode of entrance. And during the ceremony, the sea became still and there was no wind, and it seemed that all things were hushed in awful expectation of the nameless visitor. But after all was done, and the last word had been repeated by Oigos and me, we stood and waited vainly for a visible sign or other manifestation. The lamps burned stilly in the midnight room; and no shadows fell, other than were cast by ourselves and Oigos and by the great marble women along the walls. And in the magic mirrors we had placed cunningly, to reflect those that were otherwise unseen, we beheld no breath or trace of any image.

At this, after a reasonable interim, Avyctes was sorely disappointed, deeming that the evocation had failed of its purpose; and I, having the same thought, was secretly relieved. And we questioned the mummy of Oigos, to learn if he had perceived in the room, with such senses as are peculiar to the dead, the sure token or doubtful proof of a presence undescried by us the living. And the mummy gave a necromantic answer, saying that there was nothing.

"Verily," said Avyctes, "it were useless to wait longer. For surely in some way we have misunderstood the purport of the writing, or have failed to duplicate the matters used in the evocation, or the correct intonement of the words. Or it may be that in the lapse of so many aeons, the thing that was formerly wont to respond has long ceased to exist, or has altered in its attributes so that the spell is now void and valueless." To this I assented readily, hoping that the matter was at an end. So, after erasing the blood-marked triangle and the sacred ellipse of the linked Signs of Oumor, and after dismissing Oigos to his wonted place among other mummies, we retired to sleep. And in the days that followed, we resumed our habitual studies, but made no mention to each other of the strange triangular tablet or the vain formula.

Even as before, our days went on; and the sea climbed and roared in white fury on the cliffs, and the winds wailed by in their unseen, sullen wrath, bowing the dark cedars as witches are bowed by the breath of Taaran, god of evil. Almost, in the marvel of new tests and cantraips, I forgot the ineffectual conjuration, and I deemed that Avyctes had also forgotten it.

All things were as of yore, to our sorcerous perception; and there was naught to trouble us in our wisdom and power and serenity, which we deemed secure above the sovereignty of kings. Reading the horoscopic stars, we found no future ill in their aspect; nor was any shadow of bale foreshown to us through geomancy, or other modes of divination such as we employed. And our familiars, though grisly and dreadful to mortal gaze, were wholly obedient to us the masters.

Then, on a clear summer afternoon, we walked, as was often our custom, on the marble terrace behind the house. In robes of ocean-purple, we paced among the windy trees with their blown, crooked shadows; and there, following us as we went to and fro, I saw the blue shadow of Avyctes and my own shadow on the marble; and between them, an adumbration that was not wrought by any of the cedars. And I was greatly startled, but spoke not of the matter to Avyctes, and observed the unknown shadow with covert care.

I saw that it followed closely the shadow of Avyctes, keeping ever the same distance. And it fluttered not in the wind, but moved with a flowing as of some heavy, thick, putrescent liquid; and its color was not blue nor purple nor black, nor any other hue to which man's eyes are habituated, but a hue as of some unearthly purulence; and its form was altogether monstrous, having a squat head and a long, undulant body, without similitude to beast or devil.

Avyctes heeded not the shadow; and still I feared to speak, though I thought it an ill thing for the master to be companioned thus. And I moved closer to him, in order to detect by touch or other perception the invisible presence that had cast the adumbration. But the air was void to sunward of the shadow; and I found nothing opposite the sun nor in any oblique direction, though I searched closely, knowing that certain beings cast their shadows thus.

After a while, at the customary hour, we returned by the coiling stairs and monster-flanked portals into the high house. And I saw that the strange adumbration moved ever behind the shadow of Avyctes, falling horrible and unbroken on the steps and passing clearly separate and distinct amid the long umbrages of the towering monsters. And in the dim halls beyond the sun, where shadows should not have been, I beheld with terror the distorted loathly blot, having a pestilent, unnamable hue, that followed Avyctes as if in lieu of his own extinguished shadow. And all that day, everywhere that we went, at the table served by specters, or in the mummy-warded room of volumes and books, the thing pursued Avyctes, clinging to him even as leprosy to the leper. And still the master had perceived it not; and still I forbore to warn him, hoping that the visitant would withdraw in its own time, going obscurely as it had come.

But at midnight, when we sat together by the silver lamps, pondering the blood-writ runes of Hyperborea, I saw that the shadow had drawn closer to the shadow of Avyctes, towering behind his chair on the wall between the huge sculptured women and the mummies. And the thing was a streaming ooze of charnel pollution, a foulness beyond the black leprosies of hell; and I could bear it no more; and I cried out in my fear and loathing, and informed the master of its presence.

Beholding now the shadow, Avyctes considered it closesly and in silence; and there was neither fear nor awe nor abhorrence in the deep, graven wrinkles of his visage. And he said to me at last:

"This thing is a mystery beyond my lore; but never, in all the practice of my art, has any shadow come to me unbidden. And since all others of our evocations have found answer ere this, I must deem that the shadow is a veritable entity, or the sign of an entity, that has come in belated response to the formula of the serpent-sorcerers, which we thought powerless and void. And I think it well that we should now repair to the chamber of conjuration, and interrogate the shadow in such manner as we may, to inquire its nativity and purpose."

We went forthwith into the chamber of conjuration, and made such preparations as were both necessary and possible. And when we were prepared to question it, the unknown shadow had drawn closer still to the shadow of Avyctes, so that the clear space between the two was no wider than the thickness of a necromancer's rod.

Now, in all ways that were feasible, we interrogated the shadow, speaking through our own lips and the lips of mummies and statues. But there was no determinable answer; and calling certain of the devils and phantoms that were our familiars, we made question through the mouths of these, but without result. And all the while, our magic mirrors were void of any reflection of a presence that might have cast the shadow; and they that had been our spokesmen could detect nothing in the room. And there was no spell, it seemed, that had power upon the visitant. So Avyctes became troubled; and drawing on the floor with blood and ashes the ellipse of Oumor, wherein no demon nor spirit may intrude, he retired to its center. But still within the ellipse, like a flowing taint of liquid corruption, the shadow followed his shadow; and the space between the two was no wider than the thickness of a wizard's pen.

Now, on the face of Avyctes, horror had graven new wrinkles; and his brow was beaded with a deathly sweat. For he knew, even as I, that this was a thing beyond all laws, and foreboding naught but disaster and evil. And he cried to me in a shaken voice, and said:

"I have no knowledge of this thing nor its intention toward me, and no power to stay its progress. Go forth and leave me now; for I would not that any man should witness the defeat of my sorcery and the doom that may follow thereupon. Also, it were well to depart while there is time, lest you too should become the quarry of the shadow and be compelled to share its menace."

Though terror had fastened upon my inmost soul, I was loath to leave Avyctes. But I had sworn to obey his will at all times and in every respect; and moreover I knew myself doubly powerless against the adumbration, since Avyctes himself was impotent.

So, bidding him farewell, I went forth with trembling limbs from the haunted chamber; and peering back from the threshold, I saw that the alien umbrage, creeping like a noisome blotch on the floor, had touched the shadow of Avyctes. And at that moment the master shrieked aloud like one in nightmare; and his face was no longer the face of Avyctes but was contorted and convulsed like that of some helpless madman who wrestles with an unseen incubus. And I looked no more, but fled along the dim outer hall and through the high portals giving upon the terrace.

A red moon, ominous and gibbous, had declined above the terrace and the crags; and the shadows of the cedars were elongated in the moon; and they wavered in the gale like the blown cloaks of enchanters. And stooping against the gale, I fled across the terrace toward the outer stairs that led to a steep path in the riven waste of rocks and chasms behind Avyctes' house. I neared the terrace edge, running with the speed of fear; but I could not reach the topmost outer stair; for at every step the marble flowed beneath me, fleeing like a pale horizon before the seeker. And though I raced and panted without pause, I could draw no nearer to the terrace edge.

At length I desisted, seeing that an unknown spell had altered the very space about the house of Avyctes, so that none could escape therefrom to landward. So, resigning myself in despair to whatever might befall, I returned toward the house. And climbing the white stairs in the low, level beams of the crag-caught moon, I saw a figure that awaited me in the portals. And I knew by the trailing robe of sea-purple, but by no other token, that the figure was Avyctes. For the face was no longer in its entirety the face of man, but was become a loathly fluid amalgam of human features with a thing not to be identified on earth. The transfiguration was ghastlier than death or the changes of decay; and the face was already hued with the nameless, corrupt and purulent color of the strange shadow, and had taken on, in respect to its outlines, a partial likeness to the squat profile of the shadow. The hands of the figure were not those of any terrene being; and the shape beneath the robe had lengthened with a nauseous undulant pliancy; and the face and fingers seemed to drip in the moonlight with a deliquescent corruption. And the pursuing umbrage, like a thickly flowing blight, had corroded and distorted the very shadow of Avyctes, which was now double in a manner not to be narrated here.

Fain would I have cried or spoken aloud; but horror had dried up the fount of speech. And the thing that had been Avyctes beckoned me in silence, uttering no word from its living and putrescent lips. And with eyes that were no longer eyes, but had become an oozing abomination, it peered steadily upon me. And it clutched my shoulder closely with the soft leprosy of its fingers, and led me half-swooning with revulsion along the hall, and into that room where the mummy of Oigos, who had assisted us in the threefold incantation of the serpent-men, was stationed with several of his fellows.

By the lamps which illumed the chamber, burning with pale, still, perpetual flames, I saw that the mummies stood erect along the wall in their exanimate repose, each in his wonted place with his tall shadow beside him. But the great, gaunt shadow of Oigos on the marble wall was companioned by an adumbration similar in all respects to the evil thing that had followed the master and was now incorporate with him. I remembered that Oigos had performed his share of the ritual, and had repeated an unknown stated word in turn after Avyctes; and so I knew that the horror had come to Oigos in turn, and would wreak itself upon the dead even as on the living. For the foul, anonymous thing that we had called in our presumption could manifest itself to mortal ken in no other way than this.

We had drawn it from unfathomable depths of time and space, using igno-rantly a dire formula; and the thing had come at its own chosen hour, to stamp itself in abomination uttermost on the evocators.

Since then, the night has ebbed away, and a second day has gone by like a sluggish ooze of horror. . . . I have seen the complete identification of the shadow with the flesh and the shadow of Avyctes . . . and also I have seen the slow encroachment of that other umbrage, mingling itself with the lank shadow and the sere, bituminous body of Oigos, and turning them to a similitude of the thing which Avyctes has become. And I have heard the mummy cry out like a living man in great pain and fear, as with the throes of a second dissolution, at the impingement of the shadow. And long since it has grown silent, like the other horror, and I know not its thoughts or its intent. . . . And verily I know not if the thing that has come to us be one or several; nor if its avatar will rest complete with the three that summoned it forth into time, or be extended to others.

But these things, and much else, I shall soon know; for now, in turn, there is a shadow that follows mine, drawing ever closer. The air congeals and curdles with an unseen fear; and they that were our familiars have fled from the mansion; and the great marble women seem to tremble where they stand along the walls. But the horror that was Avyctes, and the second horror that was Oigos, have left me not, and neither do they tremble. And with eyes that are not eyes, they seem to brood and watch, waiting till I too shall become as they. And their stillness is more terrible than if they had rended me limb from limb. And there are strange voices in the wind, and alien roarings upon the sea; and the walls quiver like a thin veil in the black breath of remote abysses.

So, knowing that the time is brief, I have shut myself in the room of volumes and books and have written this account. And I have taken the bright triangular tablet, whose solution was our undoing, and have cast it from the window into the sea, hoping that none will find it after us. And now I must make an end, and enclose this writing in the sealed cylinder of orichalchum, and fling it forth to drift upon the wave. For the space between my shadow and the shadow of the horror is straitened momently. . . . and the space is no wider than the thickness of a wizard's pen.

A NIGHT IN MALNÉANT

My sojourn in the city of Malnéant occurred during a period of my life no less dim and dubious than that city itself and the misty regions lying there about. I have no precise recollection of its locality, nor can I remember exactly when and how I came to visit it. But I had heard vaguely that such a place was situated along my route; and when I came to the fog-enfolded river that flows beside its walls, and heard beyond the river the mortuary tolling of many bells, I surmised that I was approaching Malnéant.

On reaching the gray, colossal bridge that crosses the river, I could have continued at will on other roads leading to remoter cities: but it seemed to me that I might as well enter Malnéant as any other place. And so it was that I set foot on the bridge of shadowy arches, under which the black waters flowed in stealthy division and were joined again in a silence as of Styx and Acheron.

That period of my life, I have said, was dim and dubious: all the more so, mayhap, because of my need for forgetfulness, my persistent and at times partially rewarded search for oblivion. And that which I needed to forget above all was the death of the lady Mariel, and the fact that I myself had slain her as surely as if I had done the deed with my own hand. For she had loved me with an affection deeper and purer and more stable than mine; and my changeable temper, my fits of cruel indifference or ferocious irritability, had broken her gentle heart. So it was that she had sought the anodyne of a lethal poison; and after she was laid to rest in the somber vaults of her ancestors, I had become a wanderer, followed and forever tortured by a belated remorse. For months, or years, I am uncertain which, I roamed from old-world city to city, heeding little where I went if only wine and the other agents of oblivion were available. . . . And thus I came, some while in my indefinite journeying, to the dim environs of Malnéant.

The sun (if ever there was a sun above this region) had been lost for I knew not how long in a sky of leaden vapors; the day was drear and sullen at best. But now, by the thickening of the shadows and the mist, I felt that evening must be near; and the bells I had heard, however heavy and sepulchral their tolling, gave at least the assurance of prospective shelter for the night. So I crossed the long bridge and entered the grimly yawning gate with a quickening of my footsteps even if with no alacrity of spirit.

The dusk had gathered behind the gray walls, but there were few lights in the city. Few people were abroad, and these went upon their way with a sort of solemn haste, as if on some funereal errand that would permit no delay. The streets were narrow, the houses high, with overhanging balconies and heavily curtained or shuttered windows. All was very silent, except for the bells, which tolled recurrently, sometimes faint and far off, and sometimes with a loud and startling clangor that seemed to come almost from overhead.

As I plunged among the shadowy mansions, along the streets from which a visible twilight issued to envelop me, it seemed that I was going farther and farther away from my memories at every step. For this reason I did not at once inquire my way to a tavern but was content to lose myself more and more in the gray labyrinth of buildings, which grew vaguer and vaguer amid the ever-mounting darkness and fog, as if they were about to dissolve in oblivion.

I think that my soul would have been almost at peace with itself, if it had not been for the reiterant ringing of the bells, which were like all bells that toll for the repose of the dead, and therefore set me to remembering those that had rung for Mariel. But whenever they ceased, my thoughts would drift back with an indolent ease, a recovered security, to the all-surrounding vagueness . . .

I had no idea how far I had gone in Malnéant, nor how long I had roamed among those houses that hardly seemed as if they could be peopled by any but the sleeping or the dead. At last, however, I became aware that I was very tired, and bethought me of food and wine and a lodging for the night. But nowhere in my wanderings had I noticed the sign-board of an inn; so I resolved to ask the next passer-by for the desired direction.

As I have said before, there were few people abroad. Now, when I made up my mind to address one of them, it appeared that there was no one at all; and I walked onward through street after street in my futile search for a living face.

At length I met two women, clothed in gray that was cold and dim as the folds of the fog, and veiled withal, who were hurrying along with the same funereal intentness I had perceived in all other denizens of that city. I made bold to accost them, asking if they could direct me to an inn.

Scarcely pausing or even turning their heads, they answered: "We cannot tell you. We are shroud-weavers, and we have been busy making a shroud for the lady Mariel."

Now, at that name, which of all names in the world was the one I should least have expected or cared to hear, an unspeakable chill invaded my heart, and a dreadful dismay smote me like the breath of the tomb. It was indeed strange that in this dim city, so far in time and space from all I had fled to escape, a woman should have recently died who was also named Mariel. The coincidence appeared so sinister that an odd fear of the streets through which I had wandered was born suddenly in my soul. The name had evoked, with a more irrevocable fatality than the tolling of the bells, all that I had vainly wished to forget; and my memories were like living coals in my heart.

As I went onward, with paces that had become more hurried, more feverish than those of the people of Malnéant, I met two men, who were likewise dressed from head to foot in gray; and I asked of them the same question I had asked of the shroud-weavers.

"We cannot tell you," they replied. "We are coffin-makers, and we have been busy making a coffin for the lady Mariel."

As they spoke, and hastened on, the bells rang out again, this time very near at hand, with a more dismal and sepulchral menace in their leaden tolling. And everything about me, the tall and misty houses, the dark, indefinite streets, the rare and wraith-like figures, became as if part of the obscure confusion and fear and bafflement of a nightmare. Moment by moment, the coincidence on which I had stumbled appeared all too bizarre for belief, and I was troubled now by the monstrous and absurd idea that the Mariel I knew had only just died, and that this fantastic city was in some unsurmisable manner connected with her death. But this, of course, my reason rejected summarily, and I kept repeating to myself: "The Mariel of whom they speak is another Marel." And it irritated me beyond all measure that a thought so enormous and ludicrous should return when my logic had dismissed it.

I met no more people of whom to inquire my way. But at length, as I fought with my shadowy perplexity and my burning memories, I found that I had paused beneath the weather-beaten sign of an inn, on which the lettering had been half effaced by time and the brown lichens. The building was obviously very old, like all the houses in Malnéant; its upper stories were lost in the swirling fog, except for a few furtive lights that glowed obscurely down; and a vague and musty odor of antiquity came forth to greet me as I mounted the steps and tried to open the ponderous door. But the door had been locked or bolted; so I began to pound upon it with my fists to attract the attention of those within.

After much delay, the door was opened slowly and grudgingly, and a cadaverous-looking individual peered forth, frowning with portentous gravity as he saw me.

"What do you desire?" he queried, in tones that were both brusk and solemn.

"A room for the night, and wine," I requested.

"We cannot accommodate you. All the rooms are occupied by people who have come to attend the obsequies of the lady Mariel; and all the wine in the house has been requisitioned for their use. You will have to go else-where."

He closed the door quickly upon me with the last words. I turned to resume my wanderings, and all that had troubled me before was now intensified a hundredfold. The gray mists and the grayer houses were full of the menace of memory: they were like traitorous tombs from which the cadavers of dead hours poured forth to assail me with envenomed fangs and talons. I cursed the hour when I had entered Malnéant, for it seemed to me now that in so doing I had merely completed a funereal, sinister circle through time, and had returned to the day of Mariel's death. And certainly, all my recollections of Mariel, of her final agony and her entombment, had assumed the frightful vitality of present things. But my reason still maintained, of course, that the Mariel who lay dead somewhere in Malnéant, and for whom all these obsequial preparations were being made, was not the lady whom I had loved, but another.

After threading streets that were even darker and narrower than those before traversed, I found a second inn, bearing a similar weather-beaten sign, and in all other respects very much like the first. The door was barred, and I knocked thereon with trepidation and was in no manner surprised when a second individual with a cadaverous face informed me in tones of sepulchral solemnity:

"We cannot accommodate you. All the rooms have been taken by musicians and mourners who will serve at the obsequies of the lady Mariel; and all the wine has been reserved for their use."

Now I began to dread the city about me with a manifold fear: for apparently the whole business of the people in Malnéant consisted of preparations for the funeral of this lady Mariel. And it began to be obvious that I must walk the streets of the city all night because of these same preparations. All at once, an overwhelming weariness was mingled with my night-mare terror and perplexity.

I had not long continued my peregrinations, after leaving the second inn, when the bells were tolled once more. For the first time, I found it possible to identify their source: they were in the spires of a great cathedral which loomed immediately before me through the fog. Some people were entering the cathedral, and a curiosity, which I knew to be both morbid and perilous, prompted me to follow them. Here, I somehow felt, I should be able to learn more regarding the mystery that tormented me.

All was dim within, and the light of many tapers scarcely served to illumine the vast nave and altar. Masses were being said by priests in black whose faces I could not see distinctly; and to me, their chanting was like words in a dream; and I could hear nothing, and nothing was plainly visible in all the place, except a bier of opulent fabrics on which there lay a motionless form in white. Flowers of many hues had been strewn upon the bier, and their fragrance filled the air with a drowsy languor, with an anodyne that seemed to drug my heart and brain. Such flowers had been cast on the bier of Mariel; and even thus, at her funeral, I had been over-come by a momentary dulling of the senses because of their perfume.

Dimly I became aware that someone was at my elbow. With eyes still intent on the bier, I asked:

"Who is it that lies yonder, for whom these masses are being said and these bells are rung?" And a slow, sepulchral voice replied:

"It is the lady Mariel, who died yesterday and who will be interred tomorrow in the vaults of her ancestors. If you wish, you may go forward and gaze upon her."

So I went down the cathedral aisle, even to the side of the bier, whose opulent fabrics trailed on the cold flags. And the face of her who lay thereon, with a tranquil smile upon the lips, and tender shadows upon the shut eyelids, was the face of the Mariel I had loved and of none other. The tides of time were frozen in their flowing; and all that was or had been or could be, all of the world that existed aside from her, became as fading shadows; and even as once before (was it eons or instants ago?) my soul was locked in the marble hell of its supreme grief and regret. I could not move, I could not cry out nor even weep, for my very tears were turned to ice. And now I knew with a terrible certitude that this one event, the death of the lady Mariel, had drawn apart from all other happenings, had broken away from the sequence of time and had found for itself a setting of appropriate gloom and solemnity; or perhaps had even built around itself the whole enormous maze of that spectral city, in which to abide my destined return among the mists of a deceptive oblivion.

At length, with an awful effort of will, I turned my eyes away; and leaving the cathedral with steps that were both hurried and leaden, I sought to find an egress from the dismal labyrinth of Malnéant to the gate by which I had entered. But this was by no means easy, and I must have roamed for hours in alleys blind and stifling as tombs, and along the tortuous, self-reverting thoroughfares, ere I came to a familiar street and was able henceforward to direct my paces with something of surety. And a dull and sunless daylight was dawning behind the mists when I crossed the bridge and came again to the road that would lead me away from that fatal city.

Since then, I have wandered long and in many places. But never again have I cared to revisit those old-world realms of fog and mist, for fear that I should come once more to Malnéant, and find that its people are still busied with their preparations for the obsequies of the lady Mariel.

THE DEVOTEE OF EVIL

The old larcom house was a mansion of considerable size and dignity, set among oaks and cypresses on the hill behind Auburn's Chinatown, in what had once been the aristocratic section of the village. At the time of which I write, it had been unoccupied for several years and had begun to present the signs of desolation and dilapidation which untenanted houses so soon display. The place had a tragic history and was believed to be haunted. I had never been able to procure any first-hand or precise accounts of the spectral manifestations that were accredited to it. But certainly it possessed all the necessary antecedents of a haunted house. The first owner, Judge Peter Larcom, had been murdered beneath its roof back in the seventies by a maniacal Chinese cook; one of his daughters had gone insane; and two other members of the family had died accidental deaths. None of them had prospered: their legend was one of sorrow and disaster.

Some later occupants, who had purchased the place from the one surviving son of Peter Larcom, had left under circumstances of inexplicable haste after a few months, moving permanently to San Francisco. They did not return even for the briefest visit; and beyond paying their taxes, they gave no attention whatever to the place. Everyone had grown to think of it as a sort of historic ruin, when the announcement came that it had been sold to Jean Averaud, of New Orleans.

My first meeting with Averaud was strangely significant, for it revealed to me, as years of acquaintance would not necessarily have done, the peculiar bias of his mind. Of course, I had already heard some odd rumors about him; his personality was too signal, his advent too mysterious, to escape the usual fabrication and mongering of village tales. I had been told that he was extravagantly rich, that he was a recluse of the most eccentric type, that he had made certain very singular changes in the inner structure of the old house; and last, but not least, that he lived with a beautiful mulatress who never spoke to anyone and who was believed to be his mistress as well as his housekeeper. The man himself had been described to me by some as an unusual but harmless lunatic, and by others as an all-round Mephistopheles.

I had seen him several times before our initial meeting. He was a sallow, saturnine Creole, with the marks of race in his hollow cheeks and feverish eyes. I was struck by his air of intellect, and by the fiery fixity of his gaze—the gaze of a man who is dominated by one idea to the exclusion of all else. Some medieval alchemist, who believed himself to be on the point of attaining his objective after years of unrelenting research, might have looked as he did.

I was in the Auburn library one day when Averaud entered. I had taken a newspaper from one of the tables and was reading the details of an atrocious crime—the murder of a woman and her two infant children by the husband and father, who had locked his victims in a clothes-closet, after saturating their garments with oil. He had left the woman's apron-string caught in the shut door, with the end protruding, and had set fire to it like a fuse.

Averaud passed the table where I was reading. I looked up, and saw his glance at the headlines of the paper I held. A moment later he returned and sat down beside me, saying in a low voice:

"What interests me in a crime of that sort is the implication of unhuman forces behind it. Could any man, on his own initiative, have conceived and executed anything so gratuitously fiendish?"

"I don't know," I replied, somewhat surprised by the question and by my interrogator. "There are terrifying depths in human nature—more abhorrent than those of the jungle."

"I agree. But how could such impulses, unknown to the most brutal progenitors of man, have been implanted in his nature, unless through some ulterior agency?"

"You believe, then, in the existence of an evil force or entity—a Satan or an Ahriman?"

"I believe in evil—how can I do otherwise when I see its manifestations everywhere? I regard it as an all-controlling power; but I do not think that the power is personal in the sense of what we know as personality. A Satan? No. What I conceive is a sort of dark vibration, the radiation of a black sun, of a center of malignant eons—a radiation that can penetrate like any other ray—and perhaps more deeply. But probably I don't make my meaning clear at all."

I protested that I understood him; but, after his burst of communicativeness, he seemed oddly disinclined to pursue the conversation. Evidently he had been prompted to address me; and no less evidently, he regretted having spoken with so much freedom. He arose; but before leaving, he said:

"I am Jean Averaud—perhaps you have heard of me. You are Philip Hastane, the novelist. I have read your books and I admire them. Come and see me sometime—we may have certain tastes in common."

Averaud's personality, the conception he had avowed, and the intense interest and value which he so obviously attached to these conceptions, made a singular impression on my mind, and I could not forget him. When, a few days later, I met him on the street and he repeated his invitation with a cordialness that was unfeignedly sincere, I could do no less than accept. I was interested, though not altogether attracted, by his bizarre, well-nigh morbid individuality, and was impelled by a desire to learn more concerning him. I sensed a mystery of no common order—a mystery with elements of the abnormal and the uncanny.

The grounds of the old Larcom place were precisely as I remembered them, though I had not found occasion to pass them for some time. They were a veritable tangle of Cherokee rose-vines, arbutus, lilac, ivy and crepe-myrtle, half overshadowed by the great cypresses and somber evergreen oaks. There was a wild, half-sinister charm about them—the charm of rampancy and ruin. Nothing had been done to put the place in order, and there were no outward repairs in the house itself, where the white paint of bygone years was being slowly replaced by mosses and lichens that flourished beneath the eternal umbrage of the trees. There were signs of decay in the roof and pillars of the front porch; and I wondered why the new owner, who was reputed to be so rich, had not already made the necessary restorations.

I raised the gargoyle-shaped knocker and let it fall with a dull, lugubrious clang. The house remained silent; and I was about to knock again, when the door opened slowly and I saw for the first time the mulatress of whom so many village rumors had reached me.

The woman was more exotic than beautiful, with fine, mournful eyes and bronze-colored features of a semi-negroid irregularity. Her figure, though, was truly perfect, with the curving lines of a lyre and the supple grace of some feline animal. When I asked for Jean Averaud, she merely smiled and made signs for me to enter. I surmised at once that she was dumb.

Waiting in the gloomy library to which she conducted me, I could not refrain from glancing at the volumes with which the shelves were congested. They were an ungodly jumble of tomes that dealt with anthropology, ancient religions, demonology, modern science, history, psychoanalysis and ethics. Interspersed with these were a few romances and volumes of poetry. Beausobre's monograph on Manichaeism was flanked with Byron and Poe; and *Les Fleurs du Mal* jostled a late treatise on chemistry.

Averaud entered, after several minutes, apologizing profusely for his delay. He said that he had been in the midst of certain labors when I came; but he did not specify the nature of these labors. He looked even more hectic and fiery-eyed than when I had seen him last. He was patently glad to see me, and eager to talk.

"You have been looking at my books," he observed immediately. "Though you might not think so at first glance, on account of their seeming diversity, I have selected them all with a single object: the study of evil in all its aspects, ancient, medieval and modern. I have traced it in the religions and demonologies of all peoples; and, more than this, in human history itself. I have found it in the inspiration of poets and romancers who have dealt with the darker impulses, emotion and acts of man. Your novels have interested me for this reason: you are aware of the baneful influences which surround us, which so often sway or actuate us. I have followed the working of these agencies even in chemical reactions, in the growth and decay of trees, flowers, minerals. I feel that the processes of physical decomposition, as well as the similar mental and moral processes, are due entirely to them.

"In brief, I have postulated a monistic evil, which is the source of all death, deterioration, imperfection, pain, sorrow, madness and disease. This evil, so feebly counteracted by the powers of good, allures and fascinates me above all things. For a long time past, my life-work has been to ascertain its true nature, and trace it to its fountain-head. I am sure that somewhere in space there is the center from which all evil emanates."

He spoke with a wild air of excitement, of morbid and semimaniacal intensity. His obsession convinced me that he was more or less unbalanced; but there was an unholy logic in the development of his ideas; and I could not but recognize a certain disordered brilliancy and range of intellect.

Scarcely waiting for me to reply, he continued his monologue:

"I have learned that certain localities and buildings, certain arrangements of natural or artificial objects, are more favorable to the reception of evil influences than others. The laws that determine the degree of receptivity are still obscure to me; but at least I have verified the fact itself. As you know, there are houses or neighborhoods notorious for a succession of crimes or misfortunes; and there are also articles, such as certain jewels, whose possession is accompanied by disaster. Such places and things are receivers of evil . . . I have a theory, however, that there is always more or less interference with the direct flow of the malignant force; and that pure, absolute evil has never yet been manifested.

"By the use of some device which would create a proper field or form a receiving station, it should be possible to evoke this absolute evil. Under such conditions, I am sure that the dark vibration would become a visible and tangible thing, comparable to light or electricity." He eyed me with a gaze that was disconcertingly exigent. Then:

"I will confess that I have purchased this old mansion and its grounds mainly on account of their baleful history. The place is unusually liable to the influences of which I have spoken. I am now at work on an apparatus by means of which, when it is perfected, I hope to manifest in their essential purity the radiations of malign force."

At this moment, the mulatress entered and passed through the room on some household errand. I thought that she gave Averaud a look of maternal tenderness, watchfulness and anxiety. He, on his part seemed hardly to be aware of her presence, so engrossed was he in the strange ideas and the stranger project he had been expounding. However, when she had gone, he remarked:

"That is Fifine, the one human being who is really attached to me. She is mute, but highly intelligent and affectionate. All my people, an old Louisiana family, are long departed . . . and my wife is doubly dead to me." A spasm of obscure pain contracted his features, and vanished. He resumed his monologue; and at no future time did he again refer to the presumably tragic tale at which he had hinted: a tale in which, I sometimes suspect, were hidden the seeds of the strange moral and mental perversion which he was to manifest more and more.

I took my leave, after promising to return for another talk. Of course, I considered now that Averaud was a madman; but his madness was of a most uncommon and picturesque variety. It seemed significant that he should have chosen me for a confidant. All others who met him found him uncommunicative and taciturn to an extreme degree. I suppose he had felt the ordinary human need of unburdening himself to someone; and had selected me as the only person in the neighborhood who was potentially sympathetic.

I saw him several times during the month that followed. He was indeed a strange psychological study; and I encouraged him to talk without reserve—though such encouragement was hardly necessary. There was much that he told me—a strange medley of the scientific and the mystic. I assented tactfully to all that he said, but ventured to point out the possible dangers of his evocative experiments, if they should prove successful. To this, with the fervor of an alchemist or a religious devotee, he replied that it did not matter—that he was prepared to accept any and all consequences.

More than once he gave me to understand that his invention was progressing favorably. And one day he said, with abruptness:

"I will show you my mechanism, if you care to see it." I protested my eagerness to view the invention, and he led me forthwith into a room to which I had not been admitted before. The chamber was large, triangular in form, and tapestried with curtains of some sullen black fabric. It had no windows. Clearly, the internal structure of the house had been changed in making it; and all the queer village tales, emanating from carpenters who had been hired to do the work, were now explained. Exactly in the center of the room, there stood on a low tripod of brass—the apparatus of which Averaud had so often spoken.

The contrivance was quite fantastic, and presented the appearance of some new, highly complicated musical instrument. I remember that there were many wires of varying thickness, stretched on a series of concave sounding-boards of some dark, unlustrous metal; and above these, there depended from three horizontal bars a number of square, circular and triangular gongs. Each of these appeared to be made of a different material; some were bright as gold, or translucent as jade; others were black and opaque as jet. A small hammerlike instrument hung opposite each gong, at the end of a silver wire.

Averaud proceeded to expound the scientific basis of his mechanism. The vibrational properties of the gongs, he said, were designed to neutralize with their sound-pitch all other cosmic vibrations than those of evil. He dwelt at much length on this extravagant theorem, developing it in a fashion oddly lucid. He ended his peroration:

"I need one more gong to complete the instrument; and this I hope to invent very soon. The triangular room, draped in black, and without windows, forms the ideal setting for my experiment. Apart from this room, I have not ventured to make any change in the house or its grounds, for fear of deranging some propitious element or collocation of elements."

More than ever, I thought that he was mad. And, though he had professed on many occasions to abhor the evil which he planned to evoke,

I felt an inverted fanaticism in his attitude. In a less scientific age he would have been a devil-worshipper, a partaker in the abominations of the Black Mass; or would have given himself to the study and practice of sorcery. His was a religious soul that had failed to find good in the scheme of things; and lacking it, was impelled to make of evil itself an object of secret reverence.

"I fear that you think me insane," he observed in a sudden flash of clairvoyance. "Would you like to watch an experiment? Even though my invention is not completed, I may be able to convince you that my design is not altogether the fantasy of a disordered brain."

I consented. He turned on the lights in the dim room. Then he went to an angle of the wall and pressed a hidden spring or switch. The wires on which the tiny hammers were strung began to oscillate, till each of the hammers touched lightly its companion gong. The sound they made was dissonant and disquieting to the last degree—a diabolic percussion unlike anything I have ever heard, and exquisitely painful to the nerves. I felt as if a flood of finely broken glass was pouring into my ears.

The swinging of the hammers grew swifter and heavier; but, to my surprise, there was no corresponding increase of loudness in the sound. On the contrary, the clangor became slowly muted, till it was no more than an undertone which seemed to be coming from an immense depth or distance—an undertone still full of disquietude and torment, like the sobbing of far-off winds in hell, or the murmur of demonian fires on coasts of eternal ice.

Said Averaud at my elbow:

"To a certain extent, the combined notes of the gongs are beyond human hearing in their pitch. With the addition of the final gong, even less sound will be audible."

While I was trying to digest this difficult idea, I noticed a partial dimming of the light above the tripod and its weird apparatus. A vertical shaft of faint shadow, surrounded by a still fainter penumbra, was forming in the air. The tripod itself, and the wires, gongs and hammers, were now a trifle indistinct, as if seen through some obscuring veil. The central shaft and its penumbra seemed to widen; and looking down at the flood, where the outer adumbration, conforming to the room's outline, crept toward the walls, I saw that Averaud and myself were now within its ghostly triangle.

At the same time there surged upon me an intolerable depression, together with a multitude of sensations which I despair of conveying in language. My very sense of space was distorted and deformed as if some unknown dimension had somehow been mingled with those familiar to us. There was a feeling of dreadful and measureless descent, as if the floor were sinking beneath me into some nether pit; and I seemed to pass beyond the room in a torrent of swirling, hallucinative images, visible but invisible, felt but intangible, and more awful, more accurst than that hurricane of lost souls beheld by Dante.

Down, down, I appeared to go, in the bottomless and phantom hell that was impinging upon reality. Death, decay, malignity, madness, gathered in the air and pressed me down like Satanic incubi in that ecstatic horror of descent. I felt that there were a thousand forms, a thousand faces about me, summoned from the gulfs of perdition. And yet I saw nothing but the white face of Averaud, stamped with a frozen and abominable rapture as he fell beside me.

Like a dreamer who forces himself to awaken, he began to move away from me. I seemed to lose sight of him for a moment in the cloud of nameless, immaterial horrors that threatened to take on the further horror of substance. Then I realized that Averaud had turned off the switch, and that the oscillating hammers had ceased to beat on those infernal gongs. The double shaft of shadow faded in mid-air, the burden of terror and despair lifted from my nerves and I no longer felt the damnable hallucination of nether space and descent.

"My God!" I cried. "What was it?"

Averaud's look was full of a ghastly, gloating exultation as he turned to me.

"You saw and felt it, then?" he queried—"that vague, imperfect manifestation of the perfect evil which exists somewhere in the cosmos? I shall yet call it forth in its entirety, and know the black, infinite, reverse raptures which attend its epiphany."

I recoiled from him with an involuntary shudder. All the hideous things that had swarmed upon me beneath the cacophonous beating of those accursed gongs drew near again for an instant; and I looked with fearful vertigo into hells of perversity and corruption. I saw an inverted soul, despairing of good, which longed for the baleful ecstasies of perdition. No longer did I think him merely mad: for I knew the thing which he sought and could attain; and I remembered, with a new significance, that line of Baudelaire's poem—"The hell wherein my heart delights."

Averaud was unaware of my revulsion, in his dark rhapsody. When I turned to leave, unable to bear any longer the blasphemous atmosphere of that room, and the sense of strange depravity which emanated from its owner, he pressed me to return as soon as possible.

"I think," he exulted, "that all will be in readiness before long. I want you to be present in the hour of my triumph."

I do not know what I said, nor what excuses I made to get away from him. I longed to assure myself that a world of unblasted sunlight and undefiled air could still exist. I went out; but a shadow followed me; and execrable faces leered or mowed from the foliage as I left the cypress-shaded grounds.

For days afterward I was in a condition verging upon neurotic disorder. No one could come as close as I had been to the primal effluence of evil and go thence unaffected. Shadowy noisome cobwebs draped themselves on all my thoughts, and presences of unlineamented fear, of shapeless horror, crouched in the half-lit corners of my mind but would never fully declare themselves. An invisible gulf, bottomless as Malebolge, seemed to yawn before me wherever I went.

Presently, though, my reason reasserted itself, and I wondered if my sensations in the black triangular room had not been wholly a matter of suggestion or auto-hypnosis. I asked myself if it were credible that a cosmic force of the sort postulated by Averaud could really exist; or, granting it existed, could be evoked by any man through the absurd intermediation of a musical device. The nervous terrors of my experience faded a little in memory; and, though a disturbing doubt still lingered, I assured myself that all I had felt was of purely subjective origin. Even then, it was with supreme reluctance, with an inward shrinking only to be overcome by violent resolve, that I returned to visit Averaud once more.

For an even longer period than usual, no one answered my knock.

Then there were hurrying footsteps, and the door was opened abruptly by Fifine. I knew immediately that something was amiss, for her face wore a look of unnatural dread and anxiety, and her eyes were wide, with the whites showing blankly, as if she gazed upon horrific things. She tried to speak, and made that ghastly inarticulate sound which the mute is able to make on occasion as she plucked my sleeve and drew me after her along the somber hall to the triangular room.

The door was open; and as I approached it, I heard a low, dissonant, snarling murmur, which I recognized as the sound of the gongs. It was like the voice of all the souls in a frozen hell, uttered by lips congealing slowly toward the ultimate torture of silence. It sank and sank till it seemed to be issuing from pits below the nadir.

Fifine shrank back on the threshold, imploring me with a pitiful glance to precede her . The lights were all turned on and Averaud, clad in a strange medieval costume, in a black gown and cap such as Faustus might have worn, stood near the percussive mechanism. The hammers were all beating with a frenzied rapidity; and the sound became still lower and tenser as I approached. Averaud did not seem to see me: his eyes, abnormally dilated, and flaming with infernal luster like those of one possessed, were fixed upon something in mid-air.

Again the soul-congealing hideousness, the sense of eternal falling, of myriad harpy-like incumbent horrors, rushed upon me as I looked and saw. Vaster and stronger than before, a double column of triangular shadow had materialized and was becoming more and more distinct. It swelled, it darkened, it enveloped the gong-apparatus and towered to the ceiling. The double column grew solid and opaque as ebony; and the face of Averaud, who was standing well within the broad penumbral shadow, became dim as if seen through a film of Stygian water.

I must have gone utterly mad for a while. I remember only a teeming delirium of things too frightful to be endured by a sane mind, that peopled the infinite gulf of hell-born illusion into which I sank with the hopeless precipitancy of the damned. There was a sickness inexpressible, a vertigo of redeemless descent, a pandemonium of ghoulish phantoms that reeled and swayed about the column of malign omnipotent force which presided over all. Averaud was only one more phantom in this delirium, when with arms outstretched in his perverse adoration, he stepped toward the inner column and passed into it till he was lost to view. And Fifine was another phantom when she ran by me to the wall and turned off the switch that operated those demoniacal hammers.

As one who re-emerges from a swoon, I saw the fading of the dual pillar, till the light was no longer sullied by any tinge of that satanic radiation. And where it had been, Averaud still stood beside the baleful instrument he had designed. Erect and rigid he stood, in a strange immobility; and I felt an incredulous horror, a chill awe, as I went forward and touched him with a faltering hand. For that which I saw and touched was no longer a human being but an ebon statue, whose face and brow and fingers were black as the Faust-like raiment or the sullen curtains. Charred as by sable fire, or frozen by black cold, the features bore the eternal ecstasy and pain of Lucifer in his ultimate hell of ice. For an instant, the supreme evil which Averaud had worshipped so madly, which he had summoned from the vaults of incalculable space, had made him one with itself; and passing, it had left him petrified into an image of its own essence. The form that I touched was harder than marble; and I knew that it would endure to all time as a testimony of the infinite Medusean power that is death and corruption and darkness.

Fifine had now thrown herself at the feet of the image and was clasping its insensible knees. With her frightful muted moaning in my ears, I went forth for the last time from that chamber and from that mansion. Vainly, through delirious months and madness-ridden years, I have tried to shake off the infrangible obsession of my memories. But there is a fatal numbness in my brain as if it too had been charred and blackened a little in that moment of overpowering nearness to the dark ray of the black statue that was Jean Averaud, the impress of awful and forbidden things has been set like an everlasting seal.

THE WILLOW LANDSCAPE

The picture was more than five hundred years old; and time had not changed its colors, unless to touch them with the mellow softness of ancient hours, with the gathering morbidezza of bygone things. It had been painted by a great artist of the Sung dynasty, on silk of the finest weave, and mounted on rollers of ebony tipped with silver. For twelve generations it had been one of the most cherished possessions of the forefathers of Shih Liang. And it was equally cherished by Shih Liang himself, who, like all his ancestors, was a scholar, a poet, and a lover of both art and nature. Often, in his dreamiest or most meditative moods, he would unroll the painting and gaze upon its idyllic loveliness with the feeling of one who retires to the seclusion and remoteness of a mountain-warded valley. It consoled him in a measure for the bustle and blare and intrigue of the imperial court, where he held an official post of no small honor; since he was not altogether native to such things and would have preferred, like the olden sages, the philosophic peace of a leaf-embowered hermitage.

The picture represented a pastoral scene of the most ideal and visionary beauty. In the background arose lofty mountains rendered vague by the slow withdrawal of morning mists; in the foreground there ran a little stream, descending in mimic turbulence to a tranquil lake, and crossed on its way by a rustic bridge of bamboo, more charming than if it were made of royal lacquer. Beyond the stream and around the lake were willows of vernal green more lovely and delicious than anything that was ever beheld except in vision or memory. Incomparable was their grace, ineffable their waving: they were like the willows of Shou Shan, the Taoist Paradise; and they trailed their foliage as leaning women trail their unbound hair. And partly hidden among them was a tiny hut; and a maiden dressed in peony pink and white was crossing the little bamboo bridge. But somehow the picture was more than a painting, was more than a veritable scene: it possessed the enchantment of far-off things for which the heart has longed in vain, of years and of places that are lost beyond recall. Surely the artist had mingled with its hues the diviner iris of dream or of retrospect, and the wine-sweet tears of a nostalgia long denied.

Shih Liang felt that he knew the landscape more intimately than any actual scene. Each time that he gazed upon it, his sensations were those of a returning wanderer. It became to him the cool and sequestered retreat in which he found a never-failing refuge from the weariness of his days. And though he was of an ascetic turn and had never married nor sought the company of women, the presence of the peony maiden on the bridge was by no means exceptionable: in fact, her tiny figure, with its more than mortal charm, was somehow an essential part of the composition and was no less important to its perfection than the stream, the willows, the lake, and the far-off mountains with their riven veils of mist. And she seemed to companion him in the visits and sojournings of reverie, when he would imagine himself repairing to the little hut or roaming beneath the delicate foliage.

In truth, Shih Liang had need of such refuge and of such companion-ship, illusory though they were. For, aside from his younger brother, Po Lung, a boy of sixteen, he was alone and without living relatives or comrades; and the fortunes of the family, declining through several genera-tions, had left him the heritor of many debts and little cash or property, except a number of priceless art-treasures. His life was increasingly sad, and oppressed by ill-health and poverty; for much of the stipend from his secre-tarial post at the court was necessarily devoted to the canceling of inherited obligations; and the remainder was barely enough for his own sustenance and the education of his brother.

Shih Liang was approaching middle-age; and his honorable heart was rejoicing over the payment of the last family debt, when there came a fresh stroke of misfortune. Through no fault or remissness of his own, but the machinations of an envious fellow-scholar, Shih Liang was suddenly deprived of his position and found himself without means of support. No other position offered itself; for a certain amount of unmerited disgrace was attached to the imperial dismissal. In order to procure the necessities of life, and continue his brother's education, Shih Liang was now forced to sell one by one many of the irreplaceable heirlooms, the antique carvings of jade and ivory, the rare porcelains and paintings of the ancestral collec-tion. This he did with extreme reluctance, with a sense of utter shame and profanation, such as could be felt only by a true lover of such things, and by one whose very soul was consecrated to the past and to the memory of his fathers.

The days and years went by, the collection dwindled piece by piece; and the time drew near when the studies of Po Lung would be completed, when he would be a scholar versed in all the classics and eligible for a position of both honor and profit. But, alas! the porcelains and lacquers, the jades and ivories had all been sold; and the paintings were likewise gone, all except the willow landscape so dearly cherished by Shih Liang.

A mortal and inassuageable sorrow, a dismay that was colder than the chill of death itself, entered the heart of Shih Liang when he realized the truth. It seemed to him that he could no longer live if he should sell the picture. But if he did not sell it, how could he complete the fraternal duty which he owed to Po Lung. There was but one possible course; and he sent word at once to the Mandarin Mung Li, a connoisseur who had purchased other pieces of the old collection, telling him that the willow picture was now for sale.

Mung Li had long coveted this picture. He came in person, his eyes gleaming in his fat face with the avidity of a collector who scents a bargain; and the transaction was soon concluded. The money was paid immediately; but Shih Liang begged leave to retain the picture for another day before delivering it to the mandarin. And knowing that Shih Liang was a man of honor, Mung Li assented readily to this request.

When the mandarin had gone, Shih Liang unrolled the landscape and hung it on the wall. His stipulation to Mung Li bad been prompted by the irresistible feeling that he must have one more hour of communion with the beloved scene, must repair once more in reverie to its inviolate retreat. After that, he would be as one without a home or a sanctuary; for he knew that in all the world there was nothing that could take the place of the willow picture or afford a like asylum for his dreams.

The mellowing rays of earliest eventide were sifted upon the silk volumen where it hung on the bare wall; but for Shih Liang, the painting was steeped in a light of supernal enchantment, was touched by more than the muted splendor of the falling sun. And it seemed to him that never before had the foliage been so tender with immortal spring, or the mist about the mountain so glamorous with eternally dissolving opal, or the maiden upon the rustic bridge so lovely with unfading youth. And somehow, by an unaccountable sorcery of perspective, the painting itself was larger and deeper than of yore, and had mysteriously assumed even more of reality, or the illusion of an actual place.

With unshed tears in his heart, like an exile who bids farewell to his natal valley, Shih Liang enjoyed the sorrowful luxury of looking upon the willow picture for the last time. Even as on a thousand former occasions. his fancy strayed beneath the branches and beside the mere, it inhabited the tiny hut whose roof was so tantalizingly revealed and concealed, it peered at the mountaintops from behind the trailing foliage, or paused upon the bridge to converse with the peony maiden.

And now there happened a strange and inexplicable thing. Though the sun had gone down while Shih Liang continued to gaze and dream, and a twilight had gathered in the room, the picture itself was no less plain and luminous than before, as if it were lit by another sun than that of contemporary time and space. And the landscape had grown even larger, till it seemed to Shih Liang that he was looking through an open door on the veritable scene itself.

Then, as bewilderment assailed him, he heard a whisper that was not an actual voice, but which seemed to emanate from the landscape and become audible as a thought in his inmost mind. And the whisper said:

"Because you have loved me so long and so dearly, and because your heart is native here but alien to all the world beside, it is now permitted that I should become for you the inviolable refuge of which you have dreamed, and a place wherein you can wander and abide forever."

So, with the surpassing joy of one whose fondest vision has been verified, the rapture of one who inherits the heaven of his reverie, Shih Liang passed from the twilight room into the morning picture. And the ground was soft with a flower-embroidered grass beneath his heel; and the leaves of the willows murmured in an April wind that blew from long ago; and he saw the door of the half-hidden hut as he had never seen it before except in fancy; and the peony maiden smiled and answered his greeting when he approached her; and her voice was like the speech of the willows and the blossoms.

The disappearance of Shih Liang was a matter of brief and passing concern to those who had known him. It was readily believed that his financial sorrows had driven him to suicide, probably by drowning in the great river that ran athwart the capital.

Po Lung, having received the money left by his brother from the sale of the last painting, was enabled to finish his education; and the willow landscape, which had been found hanging on the wall of Shih Liang's abode, was duly claimed by the Mandarin Mung Li, its purchaser.

Mung Li was delighted with his acquisition; but there was one detail which puzzled him considerably when he unrolled the volumen and examined it. He could remember only one figure, a maiden in pink and white, on the little bamboo bridge; and now there were two figures! Mung Li inspected the second figure with much curiosity, and was more than surprised when he noted that it had a singular resemblance to Shih Liang. But it was very tiny, like that of the maiden; and his eyes were dim from peering at so many porcelains and lacquers and paintings; so he could not be entirely sure. At any rate, the picture was very old; and he must have been mistaken about the number of the figures. However, it was undeniably peculiar.

Mung Li might have thought the matter still stranger, if he had looked more often at the painting. He might have found that the peony maiden and the person who resembled Shih Liang were sometimes engaged in other diversions than that of merely passing the time of day on the bamboo bridge!